Let[...] [...]e Dead

In Egypt, in the age of the Pharaohs, there existed a strange custom called LETTERS TO THE DEAD. After a person had died, loved ones in need of help would place in the tomb, often at great risk, a letter beseeching the dead to offer assistance. Such a letter was found in the tomb of SUM VII, placed there by the woman he loved.

MY BELOVED. I HAVE MISSED YOU SUCH THAT WORDS CANNOT DESCRIBE THE EMPTINESS WHICH FILLS MY HEART. THE GREAT HOUSE IS NEAR COMPLETION BUT THE WORK GOES SLOWLY SINCE YOUR FALL. ALREADY THE WORKERS HAVE BUILT A SMALL SHRINE AND NOW MY FATHER HAS BEGUN TO TALK OF BUILDING A GREAT MONUMENT FOR YOU WHICH WILL FACE THE RISING SUN. A MONUMENT IN THE SHAPE OF A LION. I HAVE GREAT FEAR NOW THAT YOU ARE GONE. *I PRAY THAT YOU WILL COME BACK.*

A NOVEL BY T.W. HARD

SUM VII

BALLANTINE BOOKS • NEW YORK

Grateful acknowledgment is made for permission to reprint the following:

An adaptation of an illustration on page 26 of *Secrets of the Great Pyramid* by Peter Tompkins. Copyright © 1971 by Peter Tompkins. Reprinted by permission of Harper & Row, Publishers, Inc. An adaptation of the illustration of "The Hemoglobin Molecule" by M. F. Perutz from the November 1964 issue of *Scientific American*. A quotation of two "religious utterances" on page 16 of *Ancient Egyptian Literature* by Andreina L. Becker-Colonna. Berkeley: The Regents of the University of California, 1972. A quotation from "Sphinx" from the *Concise Encyclopedia of Greek and Roman Mythology* with an introduction by Leonard Cottrell. Copyright © 1969 by William Collins and Sons, Glasgow and Follett Publishing Company, Chicago. Used by permission of Follett Publishing Company. Two passages from *A History of the English Language* (third edition) by A. C. Baugh and Thomas Cable. Copyright © 1978 by Prentice-Hall Inc., Englewood Cliffs, New Jersey.

The illustrations for the book were drawn by James W. Brodale.

Library of Congress Catalog Card Number: 78-2062

ISBN 0-345-28674-X

This edition published by arrangement with
Harper & Row, Publishers

Manufactured in the United States of America

First Ballantine Books Edition: March 1980

To Elizabeth, with affection and appreciation

The riddle of the Sphinx:

What animal is that,
Which has four feet at morning bright,
Has two at noon,
And three at night?

I

Discovery

1

I WISH I could tell you about death. I could tell you about the eighteen-year-old girl who clung to life for sixteen weeks, supported by a respirator before she finally slipped away. Or I could tell you about a ninety-one-year-old man who survived three cardiac arrests, and each time the doctors brought him back, he muttered: "Not yet. Not yet." Until one night a friend smuggled in some wine and he died with a smile on his face. Or I could tell you about the operation I watched as a first-year medical student, when the surgeon accidentally cut the pulmonary artery and, in a matter of seconds, the life of a man flowed out on the operating table.

Yet these are not stories about death. They are stories about the passing of life. If you ask me about death I can only shrug. Medical school does not teach you that. It teaches you about enzyme systems and muscle insertions and the electrical activity of the heart, but it does not teach you about death. For until now that is a question which science has always left to religion.

I know some of the things you are about to read may seem shrouded in speculation. Even now there are certain events I do not fully understand. If you have only seen brief mention of them in the news, it is because the institution and the physicians involved preferred to keep the information to themselves. The general public has a tendency to become confused over certain medical achievements. Sometimes, at least at the beginnings, it is best to avoid any unnecessary distortion.

So I appeal to you not to judge too quickly. At best

our understanding of death is extremely primitive. Yet there are secrets of immortality that we may finally have begun to unveil, secrets which man has pondered since the beginning of time.

Certainly I can claim no hand in these scientific accomplishments. My own involvement was merely that of chance, for I was a medical student at a large state university near San Francisco, drawn into the matter with no more purpose than looking for a summer job.

During the spring of my second year I had to seek an additional source of income. My father had supplied the tuition for the first two years. I had two younger brothers still in college. Word came down from my mother that the money was running low and everyone was going to have to help.

I spent one afternoon surveying the advertisements on the medical students' bulletin board. There were the usual ads. Rooms for rent. Microscopes for sale. Baby-sitters for hire. I think all medical-student bulletin boards read the same. Someone wanted a ride to L.A. Another offered hang-gliding lessons for $11.25.

In the middle of the board my eye fell upon a small typewritten card.

Student wanted. Must have completed freshman anatomy. Position open to assist with anatomical research this summer. Contact Ms. Jacobson, Dept. of Anatomy. Extension 7451.

The thought of spending the summer stuck away in some dissecting lab was not appealing. Still I knew of a classmate who had found a job working in the biochemistry lab. Everyone laughed at him until they heard he was earning a thousand dollars a month. So you can't always tell by advertisements.

I called the number listed, and Ms. Jacobson answered. She told me that there were already a dozen applicants. A professor named J. Arnold Reilly had requested summer assistance. If I was interested I could stop by. She would give no further information over the phone.

That afternoon I walked over to the lab. I found

Ms. Jacobson in a side office next to Dr. Reilly's. She was a heavyset, middle-aged woman, who wore glasses.

"You will have to fill out an application," she said. "And be sure to put down your grade average and how you did in anatomy. And we will need three references."

"Is there a chance I might speak with the professor?" I asked.

"Not today," she answered. "He's leading a dissection in the main amphitheater."

I sat down and filled out the application, then handed it to her.

"Where do I go from here?"

"We'll be reviewing all the applications soon," she answered coolly. "If Professor Reilly is interested, he'll get back to you. He insists on a very thorough screening process, you know."

I nodded. "Do you think he would mind if I watched part of the dissection?"

"No, I guess not," she answered. "But be very quiet and don't disturb him. They're filming today and he's invited a number of important guests."

There is always a funny smell around anatomy buildings. The formaldehyde used to preserve the tissues for dissection has a way of creeping into the walls so that its odor is never completely gone.

During the freshman year we spent an entire semester dissecting cadavers. Over the course of days and weeks we began to discover their most delicate structures. Yet we never knew their lives. We never knew if they were happy or depressed, how they had lived or what they had done. Somehow they reminded us that our own lives were no more permanent than theirs, that our dreams would someday be gone. We dissected the muscles and followed the arteries and studied the nerves, yet at the end of the semester we were no closer to the understanding of life than we had been at the beginning. For how had it come about and where had it gone?

Approaching the amphitheater I almost ran into four men who were coming out of the door. One of these men was Dr. Patrick Beeson, a renowned cardiac surgeon, a tall man with silver hair. He had given a lecture during our freshman year on the new frontiers of surgery on the heart.

He was saying, "We could have saved him. The aneurysm was below the renal vessels. Technically it would not have been difficult."

I assumed that he was talking about one of his patients. I had no idea that the man they were discussing was now lying on the dissection table in the main amphitheater.

I entered the door at the end of the hallway. The room was in the shape of a huge fan. A series of seats rose from a central stage to a gallery in the back. In the center was a large dissecting table surrounded by at least twenty people. At one end of the table was a pair of bare feet. The rest of the body was completely hidden by the crowd.

There was the soft whir of a motion-picture camera. A flash bulb went off. Several members of the party changed position.

At the head of the table was a man dressed in a mask and surgical gown. He wore rubber gloves. As he spoke he pointed out certain details of anatomy to the audience. The rest of the gathering appeared to be other scientists or physicians. There were few students present.

By standing on my tiptoes and peering over the shoulders of the men in front of me, I was able to see the body. A cloth towel covered the face and upper thorax. The abdominal cavity was open.

The man leading the dissection pointed inside the abdomen.

"The interesting thing about the aorta," he said, "is the rupture here running down to the bifurcation of the two iliac vessels. And notice the arteriosclerotic placking. And here is the point of rupture . . . and the cause of death . . . immediate I would say . . . blood pouring into the abdominal cavity . . . a sudden drop in pressure . . ."

In my eagerness to view the dissection I pushed into one of the men in front of me. He moved slightly to the side and I lost my balance. Stumbling I caught myself just in time. I had almost fallen directly on the body.

When I looked up, the eyes of the dissector stared directly into my own.

"Yes?" he asked sternly. All faces around the table turned toward me.

"I . . . I'm sorry, sir," I stammered.

"Indeed." The man behind the mask nodded.

I could not make out the face behind the mask. Only that the eyes were blue and the eyebrows thick. It was an extremely tense moment.

"What is your name, son?" His eyebrows arched, the eyes bored into my face.

"St. John, sir."

I have always felt indebted to him for what he said next. For an instant his eyes remained sternly fixed on mine until I thought I saw the faintest flicker of amusement.

"St. John, your enthusiasm is remarkable," he said. A low murmur of laughter spread around the table.

"I'm sorry, sir. I did not mean to interrupt . . ."

"Undoubtedly," he snorted. In another instant he turned back to the dissection and ignored my presence.

"So we think this is the cause of the king's death," he continued. "A ruptured aneurysm."

I tried to overcome my embarrassment and follow the dissection. An aneurysm is an abnormal saclike dilation of an artery, which usually occurs as a consequence of atherosclerosis. The artery begins to stretch and expand like a balloon. The condition is extremely dangerous, for the constant pulsing of the heart can further weaken the dilation until a rupture occurs. Then death is almost immediate.

But a king, I wondered. That would explain why the heart surgeon had been here. But a king of what? I could remember hearing nothing about any king in the news. And even if it was a king, why was an anatomy professor performing the autopsy instead of one of the pathologists over at the medical center?

I moved around the room until I could see the body clearly. The texture of the skin was dry and emaciated, yet the hands were well formed. On the fifth finger of the right hand was a strange and beautiful ring that had been carved from a blue-green stone in the shape of an insect or some kind of beetle. The knuckle beyond the ring was swollen and distorted, making it impossible to take off.

I recognized a graduate student who had assisted us with freshman anatomy.

"Who was this?" I whispered.

He looked at me as if it was difficult for him to believe I could be so stupid.

"Don't you know?"

I shook my head.

"Thutmose III."

I shook my head again. I still did not understand.

"A pharaoh," he said underneath his breath.

I mulled the word over in my mind. The only pharoah I had ever heard of lived in Egypt, and that was centuries ago.

"You mean an old Egyptian king?"

He nodded without taking his eyes away from the table.

"From the eighteenth dynasty," he whispered. "Three thousand years ago."

I glanced incredulously at the body. Except for the skin I had thought it might be the body of a man who had died only recently. He had arthritis. He still wore a ring. And he had died of a ruptured aneurysm.

2

A MONTH passed. When I did not hear further from the anatomy department, I assumed that they had hired someone else. A friend knew of a job working for the surgical department, and I told him I was interested. There was nothing else for me to do.

Therefore I was surprised when I received a small typewritten card in the mail, much like the advertisement I had first seen on the bulletin board.

Dear Mr. St. John:
    Would you be kind enough to call me to set up an interview with Professor Reilly concerning your job application.

                            Sincerely,

                            N. Jacobson

                                    Dept. of Anatomy
                                    Ext. 7451

It seemed inconsiderate to be notified so late in the year. But if a position was available, at least I wanted to find out what it was all about. I called Ms. Jacobson and arranged for a appointment later in the day.

I found the secretary sitting behind her desk just as she had been a month before.

"I am sorry we were not able to get back to you sooner," she said. "The professor was waiting to hear about a grant. You were one of the students he wanted to speak with personally."

I shrugged. "I never heard from you. A friend of

mine has offered me a job with the surgical department."

"Oh, dear," she exclaimed.

"Well I'm not really committed," I said. "It's just
that I have to find some work."

"I understand." She smiled. She seemed much more
polite than the first time I had spoken with her. She
offered me some coffee and asked me to sit down. A
half hour passed. In a back room someone was moving
around.

The buzzer on her intercom rang. "Tell Mr. St.
John to come in, please."

"Good luck," she said.

I walked slowly into the professor's office. Reilly
stood up from behind his desk. He was well tanned
and in his middle forties. He shook my hand with a
firm grip.

"Please sit down," he said. He stared at me for a
moment without speaking.

I glanced nervously around his office. The room
was cluttered. Books lay at all angles on the shelves.
The desk was stacked with papers. Two X rays were
illuminated on the view box along the wall.

"You look familiar."

"Yes, sir," I answered awkwardly. "I'm afraid I
was the student who almost fell on the body in the
amphitheater. I'm very sorry. I—"

"No, that's all right," he answered. "I was just trying
to place you. Tell me something about yourself."

I explained that I had gone to college at Stanford.
Majored in biology. The usual premed qualifications.

"Did you play any sports?"

"Rugby," I nodded.

He shook his head. "Insane sport. What position
did you play?"

"Wing."

"Are you fast?"

"Like lightning," I answered.

He smiled for a moment and paused to study me
again.

"Do you know anything about Menkaure or
Khaphre or Khufu?"

"No, sir."

"Do you know anything about Egypt?"

"Very little, sir."

"Do you know anything about anatomy?"

I was not sure how to answer him. "A little, sir."

He motioned to the two films illuminated along the wall.

"What can you tell me about the X rays?"

I walked over to the view box and studied them. One of the X rays was of a skull, the second of a chest.

"A fractured clavicle on the right, possibly a fractured rib. And a fracture line here along the skull."

"And how would you conclude this person died?"

"I would guess he was killed in a car accident."

"He?"

"Yes, sir."

Reilly stepped up to the view box next to me. "Do you see these two shadows here," he said. He pointed to two soft tissue densities on either side of the chest. "What do you call these?"

I blanched. "I think breasts, sir."

"Do men have breasts?"

"I may have missed that lecture, sir."

He looked at me out of the corner of his eye.

"What if I told you that this 'man with breasts,' as you call it, died many hundreds of years ago?"

"My first guess would be that she was killed in some kind of fight, skull cracked, clavicle smashed in. Possibly murdered."

Reilly nodded slowly. "No bad, St. John. Not bad. What else can you tell me from the X rays? The age? General health?"

I stared at the X rays again. "The bone looks solid. The teeth appear in good shape. I would say she was fairly young."

Reilly scowled. "Be exact, St. John. The third molars have not yet erupted. That puts her in the third decade of life. Epiphyseal lines along the clavicles, the humerus, the mandible are fully closed. So we know she is past her teens. And here at the skull. The suture closure of the sagittal and sphenofrontal areas has just begun. That puts her between twenty-two and twenty-four years. Let's say she was twenty-three. What else can you tell me about her health?"

"There is a small calcification in the left lung. It could be a carcinoma, but at her age I would consider tuberculosis or a fungus more likely."

"Excellent," Reilly answered. "And the liver?"

"Looks like a vague circular calcification. Perhaps some kind of a cyst."

"Good," Reilly answered. "In actuality it was probably an echinococcus cyst. Very prevalent in early Egypt."

The intercom buzzed and Reilly excused himself for a long-distance call. Someone was trying to get him to give a lecture at Harvard. He politely refused.

As soon as he had hung up there was another call. He had a visitor in his office, the dean of the medical school.

Reilly frowned. "I wish we had more time, St. John. I must say that your recommendations were very good. You have done well in medical school. And I am impressed with what you have shown me here. I think we would be very interested in you."

"Thank you, sir," I nodded.

"Would you be interested in going to Egypt this summer?"

The question took me completely by surprise.

"I . . . well . . . yes, sir. You mean with the job? Yes, of course."

"The university has been given a grant for the last five years to participate in some joint work with the University of Cairo," he said. "For some time we've been studying the Egyptian mummies, looking for disease processes which have afflicted man in the past. We've just recently received some very large funds to continue with this work.

"I need a student assistant who could come with us and help with the shipping crates, cataloging finds, looking up references—a lot of the little things that would make my work easier.

"The pay is not great," he added. "But I think we could offer you twenty-five dollars a day. Your travel and living expenses, of course, would be paid for."

He led me toward the door. "Why don't you think it over. It can be very hot and dusty. The work is often tedious. You might spend three weeks just taking X rays of a body in the Cairo Museum. Let Miss Jacobson know in a day or two. If you're not interested we'll have to pick one of the other applicants."

The door opened and I nearly bumped into the dean. He came bustling through the doorway as if he had something very important on his mind. The door closed behind me and the two disappeared in Reilly's office.

Ms. Jacobson stared at me.

"Well?"

"Thank you for setting up the interview."

"I'm sorry that we're so busy," she said. "He's going to Cairo soon, and there are last-minute details we've had to complete. Did you get the job?"

"I think so."

"What did he say?"

"Just to let you know in a day or two if I am interested."

"All right," she answered. "I'll hold off contacting any of the other applicants until I hear from you."

Halfway out the doorway I paused, wondering if I really needed to weigh all of the possibilities the summer might bring before making up my mind. The pay was good. I would be earning over seven hundred dollars a month plus expenses. And I already liked Professor Reilly. He seemed both a shrewd and magnetic person, for whom I had quickly gained respect. When it came down to it, I couldn't have dreamed of a better job.

Ms. Jacobson watched me over the rim of her glasses.

"Yes?"

"Look," I said, "why don't you tell the professor to sign me on."

"Good," she answered. "I'm sure he'll be delighted."

Ms. Jacobson called the next afternoon saying that the professor was having a faculty party at his house that night and wanted me to come. At the last minute

I invited a date. She was a good friend whom I had known since college.

Reilly lived in one of the large Tudor houses in a section of the campus which we called "Professors' Row." We were greeted at the front door by a servant. As we entered the hallway, I noticed a wood-paneled library. In the center of its far wall was a large photograph of the three great pyramids of Egypt. I was so taken by the picture, by the stark nakedness of the country and the three massive monuments, that I snuck into the room.

At the bottom of the photograph was the small figure of a man, an insignificant speck against the backdrop of great stone monuments. Someone had penciled in the caption, "Man Seeking Man."

The servant looked at me disapprovingly for having entered the room. Remembering my first stumbling introduction to the professor I hurried out. As I passed a table I noted a new book titled *Diseases of the Old World. A Comparative Study*. The author was our host.

The servant led us into the backyard, where there was an open bar with several tables set up for a buffet. The yard was filled with people. "A small dinner party," Reilly's secretary had said. I was beginning to learn that practically everything J. Arnold Reilly did was in a grand and glorious fashion.

The professor himself was surrounded by a large group of people. As soon as he saw us, he came over to talk. From the first we spoke like old friends.

"Bryan, how are you?" he said. "Sorry we didn't get a chance to talk more during our brief interview." Then he put his arms around both of us and escorted us into the midst of the gathering.

There were the usual faculty dignitaries. We met Dr. Beeson, the cardiac surgeon; Dr. Chapman, the dean; and a host of others. Even Ms. Jacobson was there.

The most unusual guest, however, was a huge dark man who stood apart from the rest of the crowd and seemed to prefer to remain in the shadows of a tree. He was easily over six-feet-five-inches tall and must have weighed two hundred and fifty pounds. After we had been introduced to everyone else, the professor took us over to him.

"This is Abdul," Reilly said, "a dear friend from many summers." As the huge man reached forward to shake my hand, I was impressed with his great strength. Yet he did not squeeze my hand tightly. He nodded with a broad smile. "Pleased to meet you, sir."

"Abdul has been working with the Cairo Museum for the past thirty years," the professor continued. "He knows everything about Egypt. Everything about digging. And everything about history—eh, Abdul?"

Abdul bowed and shrugged. "I am afraid I know very little about each," he answered. It occurred to me that he was perhaps the man in the lower left of the photograph in the professor's library, the man standing alone before the great pyramids.

We chatted briefly before movng on. As we left I noted that he drifted back into the shadows of a tree. The professor excused himself and asked us to make ourselves at home. He obviously had many guests to talk with. After that we lost him for the evening.

The following Monday Ms. Jacobson called to say the professor wanted to talk to me as soon as possible. I managed to find a break between classes in the early afternoon. When I arrived three other people were waiting to see him. I picked up a magazine and sat down. An hour passed before Ms. Jacobson told me to go in.

Professor Reilly stood up as I entered. "You ready to go to work?" He smiled. He had a way of making me feel that I was the only one he was interested in, even though he had a waiting room full of people.

"I suppose you have a hundred questions," he said. "I can't tell you how delighted we are that you will be with us. Abdul was favorably impressed," he laughed, "and that's the biggest hurdle of all.

"We'll be spending a month or so in very close quarters in a foreign country not always sympathetic to Americans. Because of the political situation I was quite concerned that we take someone who would be compatible. Someone we could count on."

I smiled with a touch of embarrassment. They had

obviously used criteria in the screening process that had never crossed my mind.

"The body you saw us working on back in the amphitheater was the fifth body in our study. We use the code name SUM V, standing for State University Mummy number Five. This summer we are funded to bring back one, possibly two, additional specimens for further study."

He paused. "All this making sense to you?"

I nodded. "What about the X rays of the young lady with the fractured clavicle?"

Reilly frowned. "That particular specimen was never unwrapped. We took X rays through the casket in Cairo. The hieroglyphics labeled her as an important wife of a pharaoh during the New Kingdom, but we think not. She was much too young and there was no evidence of significant jewelry in the wrappings. Probably she was murdered, hastily wrapped and stuffed into the coffin at the last minute, while some clever thieves made off with the body of the real queen and all of her jewelry."

"But that's incredible," I murmured.

"Egyptian history is full of intrigue." Reilly smiled. "And the study of the royal tombs brings out the worst of it. Bodies switched. Tombs broken into in the dead of night. Jewels stolen and tombs resealed. The priests tried faithfully to preserve the royal burials, but in the end the grave robbers almost always won out."

We were interrupted by a call over the intercom. The professor answered the telephone and spoke at length about a problem with a shipping crate. When he hung up, Ms. Jacobson reminded him that he had two more people waiting to see him. I could tell we were running out of time.

"Well, Bryan." He stood up from his chair. "I guess I had better finish up before the afternoon slips away."

He reached forward and shook my hand. "I'll be off to Cairo by the end of the week. Miss Jacobson will have plane tickets for your departure around the twenty-ninth of June. Wire us your exact arrival time so that we can meet you at the airport. I don't have much more for you to do here. Check on a few last-minute shipping details. That's about all. Call Miss Jacobson every couple of days so that we can keep in touch."

He broke into a broad smile. "See you in Cairo."

I spent the next week cramming for finals. When they were over, it took me three days to return to normal again. With a week left I checked in with Ms. Jacobson and began working on some of the shipping details the professor had mentioned. In my spare time I went to the library and read.

What a grand and fascinating civilization Egypt was! Five thousand years ago they had invented a pictorial form of writing. They had their own calendar. They had developed a highly sophisticated form of mathematics. They had discovered medicines and had specialists who treated their sick. And they constructed huge pyramids for their pharaohs, the likes of which the world had never seen.

Babylon sprang up on the banks of the Euphrates. Ancient prophets recorded the feats of Moses. A man named Alexander carved vast boundaries for the Persian Empire. Yet by the time of Christ the Egyptian civilization had already existed for three thousand years!

For hours I thumbed through the books in the library. Strange names like Crocodilopolis and Heliopolis rushed out of the pages at me. Drawings of ancient temples at Abu-Simbel and Memphis and Thebes now had special meaning. Musty statues in their silence seemed to beckon. And somehow the primitive surge of the Nile became my own pulse beat. For I was destined for a journey that would take me back to the very beginning of recorded time.

3

THERE WERE two changes on the flight to Cairo—one in New York and a second in Rome. The stops were short interludes lost in eighteen hours of flight. Steadily everything I had left behind began to fade into a memory of rushed preparations. The last two weeks had flown by. Passport, immunization, and last-minute packing all seemed in the distant past. And now as we crossed the Mediterranean, the sand-colored coast of Africa stretched across the horizon as far as the eye could see.

The day was crystal clear. Below us was the bleakest, most desolate land I had ever seen. There were no cities, no roads, no signs of civilization. The only change in colors was the shades of brown, where shadows marked some range of mountains or some great natural valley. Everything was monotonous sand-colored rock. Looking down on this land I could see what a great natural barrier it must have been to the travelers in the old days. What an incredible journey it must have been to cross it. How isolated the early pockets of civilization!

Stepping off the plane in Cairo was like moving into the vent of a blast furnace. The heat was everywhere. It rose off the concrete in shimmering waves and burned off the horizon in a lakelike mirage.

At customs I searched the faces in the crowd. Dark eyes, curved noses, brown skins everywhere. No one looked familiar, until a huge form descended upon me. A suitcase was snatched from my grip with a single sweep of a massive arm.

"Welcome, Mr. St. John," a deep voice said. "Welcome to Cairo."

It was Abdul, looking older, darker, more weathered than I remembered him from the professor's party. Now, in the bright light, I judged he was in his middle fifties. Faint traces of gray edged into his close-cropped hair. He was dressed in a khaki shirt, slacks, and a pair of open sandals.

He greeted me warmly, apologizing for the professor's absence. Reilly had some business at the museum and would meet us later in the afternoon. As we moved through customs, everyone seemed to know him. He stopped and chatted with a half dozen people. One of the inspecting agents yelled something and opened a special gate to let us pass. I followed Abdul out into a waiting car.

After an hour's ride we reached a small hotel located near the banks of the Nile. The professor had taken a large suite in one of the bigger hotels from which he did his work, and I was to be lodged in this nearby pension. After I checked in, Abdul parted, stating that he would pick me up later in the afternoon to join the professor. The jet lag and the heat had exhausted me.

I took a shower and quickly fell asleep, soon to be awakened by Abdul knocking at the door. It was four o'clock, he announced, and they were ready for tea.

These teas were a daily ritual. The professor often invited from one to a half dozen guests to discuss his research. Sometimes they were scientists, sometimes physicians, and more often than not they were a mixed bag of people which included historians, writers, and an occasional tourist.

During these periods it was always a pleasure to listen to Reilly. He was a witty conversationalist, and I would watch with great interest as he furrowed his eyebrows while pondering some problem. Then his eyes would brighten as he came upon a solution, leaving the rest of us still bewildered. Although he was an anatomist by training, his heart was really in archaeology, and he became most animated when talking about old tombs.

During these discussions Abdul always remained in the background. He rarely dined with us, usually preferring to eat by himself. Over the next month I was with him almost daily, yet he revealed so little of himself that I always wondered what he did with his time off. He would be gone for hours, only to reappear with a faint smile and some vague explanation that he had been "in town" or "visiting" his family. The professor told me later that he had a wife and six or eight children in Cairo, but I never saw them during my entire visit.

We spent some hours that first afternoon talking about tombs, burial jewels, and the art of mummification. We ate a late dinner, and then the professor insisted that I accompany him to the pyramids at Giza. He assured me that it was a sight I would not easily forget.

On reaching the Giza plateau we left our car and traveled to the base of the pyramids on foot. The heat of the day had begun to dissipate and the night air was cool. We stood for some moments in silence beneath the clear Egyptian sky.

"I often come here at night," Reilly said, "when everyone is gone. Sometimes I think you can reach out here and touch history. And yet," he paused, "there is still so much that we don't know."

I stared up at the great monuments, thinking of the centuries that had passed since they were built, trying to imagine the pain and suffering that must have gone into their creation. I wondered at the firm conviction of those ancient kings who thought that their lives were eternal and by building the pyramids they would gain immortality.

The largest of the pyramids and the sole surviving structure of the Seven Wonders of the World is the Great Pyramid of Khufu. It dominates the Giza plateau, hovering above two lesser pyramids and the Sphinx. To construct it 2,300,000 blocks had been assembled, each weighing more than two and a half tons. The pyramid rises to a height of 481 feet and covers thirteen square acres at its base. It is still one of the largest stone structures ever created by man.

When the Great Pyramid was first described by the historian Herodotus in 455 B.C., the original limestone mantle was so perfectly preserved that one could not thrust a reed between the blocks. Legend stated that it was the burial place of the Pharaoh Khufu and contained fabulous treasure. Ancient guides claimed that the body of the dead ruler was inside the pyramid lying upon an island surrounded by water. They whispered of gold and glittering jewels and strange metals which could bend and would not rust. Yet there was no opening leading into the pyramid. At the time of Herodotus the "secret" entrance to the north face was unknown and no one had ever been inside.

Because of this I had read with great interest the accounts of the first recorded penetration. In the ninth century A.D. one of the Arab caliphs decided to break into the pyramid. Gathering his best masons and stonesmiths he tried to crack the rock with hammer and chisel, but the outer casing proved too tough. Finally he came upon the idea of using heat. With large fires the masons scalded the rocks until they became red hot, then they poured cold vinegar upon them. As the stone cracked, they were able to chip out a small tunnel. Progress was incredibly slow. For weeks they dug at the rock until the air became so intolerable and the passage so constricted that they were on the point of giving up. Then one of the workmen heard a muffled sound. A huge block had fallen somewhere inside the structure.

With renewed fervor they dug in the direction of the sound. Within thirty feet they broke into a narrow passage leading into the depths of the pyramid. They scrambled down the corridor until they came to a partially finished chamber. But there was nothing there. No treasure, no sarcophagus, no findings of any kind.

Retracing their steps they followed the passage outward until they discovered a sealed "secret" doorway along the north face. Then, moving back along the passage, they discovered where the block had fallen from the ceiling. It was made of granite and seemed to be a plug which marked another passage leading upward into the heart of the pyramid.

For days they chiseled around the granite plug. They detoured around a second block and then a third. Finally their perseverance paid off. For beyond the third plug the Arabs broke into another passage. With great excitement they raced up the passageway until they came to a large chamber with a gabled roof, which they called the "Queen's Chamber." But again their hopes were thwarted, for the room was empty.

Retracing their steps they searched back through the passage. Here they found a partially hidden corridor leading upward to still another passage. Standing on each other's shoulders they gazed by flickering torch-light into a colossal gallery. Climbing upward they rushed over one another, scrambling for the top. At the end of the gallery they found a small passageway leading to still another chamber, the "King's Chamber." Here was a well-polished room with a lidless, empty sarcophagus. But the great treasure which they had anticipated was gone. There was no gold, no jewels, no evidence of a burial of any kind. The Great Pyramid of Khufu was empty!

Yet there are other theories about the Great Pyramid. Some state that it was never meant for a burial at all, but for various initiation rites. Others claim that the pyramid was built as a monument to provide accurate directions and standards of measurements. A few even speculate that the pyramid was a celestial observatory used to mark the calendar year and the movement of heavenly bodies. Perhaps it was all of these. Who would ever know?

When I asked Reilly what he believed of all this, he looked at me and smiled.

"Most archaeologists think the Great Pyramid was probably the design of one of Khufu's architects for his tomb. Perhaps grave robbers snuck out with all the treasure before the tomb was sealed. Yet we know that at the time of the Arab penetration the granite plug was intact. And what happened to the top of the granite sarcophagus in the 'King's Chamber'? If at one time it did exist, there is no way anyone could have carried it off without a gang of men. And why would grave robbers have wanted to?"

"I don't know, Bryan," he said. "I've thought about it many times. It's still one of the greatest mysteries."

The Sphinx loomed before us, eerily lit, staring off into the darkness with the Great Pyramid reaching skyward behind it.

"And the Sphinx?" I asked. "From all of my reading I could never find a satisfactory explanation for it."

Reilly chuckled. "Now you are beginning to understand some of the fascination of Egypt—eh?"

Twice during the next week I traveled out to the Great Pyramid during the daytime and scampered up the passages on all fours, marveling at the construction, feeling the smooth polish to the walls, wondering how the Arabs must have felt as they crashed from one corridor to the next, searching desperately for hidden treasure. But it was empty! And each time I returned to the hotel I had trouble sleeping at night. For hours I lay awake while questions darted like comets through my mind. And always the Sphinx seemed to hover over me, speaking in a strange tongue which I could not understand. Somewhere, somehow, there were answers, I thought. So close and yet so incredibly far away.

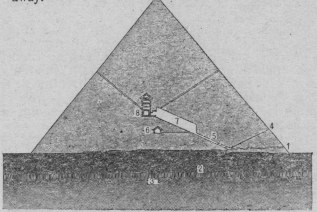

Figure 1. Chambers and passages in the Great Pyramid of Khufu (Cheops), fourth dynasty, Old Kingdom, 2700 B.C.

KEY:

1. Arab tunnel, ninth century A.D. (first recorded penetration)
2. Descending passage
3. Unfinished chamber
4. "Secret" entrance, north face
5. Ascending passage, blocked by granite plugs
6. "Queen's Chamber"
7. Grand Gallery
8. "King's Chamber"

4

DURING THE next week I spent many hours working with the professor in the Cairo Museum. A tomb had recently been discovered in the necropolis next to the pyramid complex at Giza, and he was interested in X-raying the bodies and discovering the causes of death. By the end of the week we determined that three of these bodies had broken bones and one a fractured neck. Obviously they had all come to a violent end.

Without disrupting the bodies needle biopsies of organs and various tissues were obtained for microscopic study. Tiny samples of bone were taken with a special drill. While this was done great care was taken to preserve and record all the burial jewelry. Bracelets, rings, amulets, and necklaces could all play a role in identifying the period and the possible relationships of the bodies in the tomb.

The five bodies we uncovered were not nearly as perfectly preserved as the body I had watched the professor dissect back at the university. It is interesting that the art of mummification changed considerably throughout Egypt's history.

There is evidence that the first attempts at mummification were made during the royal burials of the Old Kingdom. In these earliest graves the bodies were left intact, but the preservation techniques were crude. Unfortunately most of these remains have perished.

As the methods were gradually modified and refined, the bodies became better preserved. At the height of mummification in the New Kingdom the internal organs were removed and placed in Canopic jars, the inside of the body was washed with lye and other caustic agents, and the brains pulled out through the nose with a finely pointed hook. This process was later modified by merely forcing a toxic acid through the rectum. The acid was left for approximately seventy days and then, when the cork was pulled, so to speak, all of the insides were dissolved and washed out.

On several occasions we found small graves from the Christian era into which the bodies of certain high officials had been haphazardly thrown. In these more recent graves the bodies were left to mummify by the mere desiccation of the desert heat rather than by any elaborate, artificial means of preservation.

The professor explained during one of his afternoon teas that it was the custom of the priests to pass information by word of mouth from one generation to the next. In this way some of the most sophisticated knowledge about astronomy, pyramid-building, and mummification was kept secret from the general population. Although hieroglyphics commonly appeared on the side of temple buildings, they usually recorded little more than the feats of certain pharaohs. Often they were written in a type of script that few people could understand.

Perhaps by keeping these strange secrets to themselves the priests were able to hold their power. Reilly theorized that the entire pyramid complex at Giza was probably built at the direction of one or two savants. Without adequate records there was a gradual decay of information. As time passed each generation was forced to copy the last, leaving little opportunity for growth or experimentation.

By the end of the second week we had completed our study of the five bodies and had begun some additional work on one of the mummies in the Cairo Museum. About this time our plans changed radically. Of course it was Abdul who was primarily responsible. The knowledge that this man carried was indeed remarkable, and I should pause here to relate one small incident which involved him.

One evening I returned to the hotel and found I

could not sleep. I got up and dressed, deciding to go for a short walk. The hotel was close to the Nile and there was a small walkway which ran parallel to the river. By accident I strayed farther from the hotel than I had planned. A man came out of the shadows and introduced himself in broken English, asking if I would like a woman for the night.

On refusing I suddenly noted that he was accompanied by three others. They descended upon me, tugging on my arms and jacket, asking if I wanted to buy some "dirty" pictures. For an instant their approach threw me off guard. Then I realized that one of them was trying to get at my wallet. I twisted sideways and leaped back, but not before there was a ripping sound. When I turned around they had disappeared, but my pocket had been slit open and my wallet was gone.

Feeling very foolish I returned quickly to the hotel. The authorities, upon hearing of the robbery, merely shrugged. There was nothing they could do. I had no idea how to get my credentials back. Fortunately I had carried less than twenty pounds of Egyptian currency.

The next morning I was awakened early by Abdul. As we walked over to join the professor he handed me my wallet. Only the Egyptian money was gone. When I asked him how he came upon it, he smiled and replied that he knew the right people and cautioned me about going out at night. How he found the wallet so quickly is still a mystery to me, although I now doubt there was little which went on in that city that escaped him.

That afternoon I went over to the library to check out some reference books for the professor. When I returned he was having tea. Abdul and three other men were present, all deep in conversation. I did not interrupt but stood off in the corner and watched.

The professor's eyes were ablaze and his eyebrows arched with great excitement. The object of his interest was a piece of jewelry which had been wrapped in some matted paper and now lay upon a table.

At first glance it appeared to be the figure of a bird.

On closer inspection it proved to be a scarab with a single extended wing. The central figure was carved from a magnificent blue stone. The wing was perhaps six inches in length and composed of tiny red, blue, and green stones inlaid with gold. To my amateur eye it appeared to be of the finest workmanship. A small notch on the back of the scarab indicated where the second wing had been.

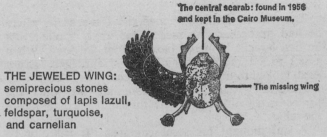

The central scarab: found in 1956 and kept in the Cairo Museum.

THE JEWELED WING: semiprecious stones composed of lapis lazuli, feldspar, turquoise, and carnelian

The missing wing

Figure 2. The Winged Scarab (rough sketch)

The professor argued for some minutes about the date of the piece, although all agreed that it was from a very early period, sometime around the reign of Khufu in the Old Kingdom 2700 B.C. On the underside of the scarab was a peculiar hieroglyph which no member of the gathering could explain.

The body of the scarab had been purchased by a museum representative a number of years before and kept in the Cairo Museum. The source of the scarab had never been traced, however, Reilly suspected that it had come from a royal tomb. It was the type of jewelry often placed upon the chest of the deceased to bring it good luck in the afterworld.

The jeweled wing had recently surfaced on the black market in Cairo. Less than a week before this wing had been purchased by a Danish tourist for two hundred pounds. The tourist had taken it to the Cairo Museum to see how valuable it was. He was astounded to discover that it was priceless, and even more astounded when the curator confiscated the wing and returned his two hundred pounds with a warning that he could be given a stiff fine for purchasing antiquities and trying to take them out of the country.

That same day the wing was carefully examined. The small blue stones which outlined the piece appeared to be a rare type of lapis lazuli. Remembering the unusual quality of the scarab the curator went back through his collection and found that the wing did indeed belong to the scarab and, in fact, formed the second of the three pieces. The last piece, the right wing, was still missing.

The curator had questioned the Dane as to where he had purchased the piece. He simply replied that he had bought it in the bazaar from an Arab. When asked to be more specific he had shrugged. Every Arab looked to him like every other.

After they had finished examining the wing, the professor asked Abdul if he thought he could locate the seller.

Abdul thought for some minutes. "It will not be easy, sir."

"How would you go about it?" Reilly asked.

I would have to take the jeweled wing and go down into the market and try to discover who might have seen it."

"Then tomorrow morning we must do this," the professor stated. "It's important that we not waste further time. If the Arab who found this piece is still in town, we must try to locate him. Perhaps he is from an outlying village and only came in to make the sale."

Abdul nodded. "I cannot guarantee anything, but we can try."

As we walked back to the hotel that night I questioned Abdul further.

"You think this jeweled wing came from a new tomb?"

Abdul shrugged. He would not commit himself.

"Possibly a new undiscovered tomb?" I persisted.

He shrugged again. "Findings like this are like gold in your country. They give rise to great hopes and speculation. So often they lead to disappointment. One should not dream. One should follow the trail methodically. If something turns up, then it is good.

Look no further than your leading foot. That is the only way."

"But it could mean that there is a new grave that no one knows about, is that right?"

Abdul placed his arm around me and smiled. "Mr. St. John, you talk too much," he said. And in a more quiet tone he added, "The tragedy will be if we have come too late."

5

HE LEFT the hotel early the following morning. Chants
of prayer from the Arab mosques drifted across the
city like faint gusts of wind. By eight o'clock we had
made our way through the traffic and into the center of
Cairo. Here, lined along the narrow streets and
packed into the side alleyways, was the gigantic market place of the Khan el-Khalili bazaar. The market
stretched for two miles, a maze of stalls, hidden streets
and dark and musty stores. Meat vendors and fish
mongers, fabric salesmen and leather workers, jewelers
and silversmiths lined the area in their little booths.
Hoarse voices called through the crowd advertising
strange and exotic goods. Naked children dashed back
and forth between the alleyways.

Abdul led, winding back and forth among the
throngs. As he pushed through the crowd we would
occasionally come to a booth where he would stop and
chat for five or ten minutes. Then he would produce
the jeweled wing from his pocket and unwrap it. The
response was always the same. The merchant would
gaze at the piece for a long time. Often he would touch
it and feel the texture of the stone with his fingers.
Almost all the vendors could tell the jewel was of great
value, for after each had finished examining it, he
would set it down carefully, almost reverently. But
none had seen it before, nor did they know where it
had come from.

At first I was completely lost. I had no idea how
Abdul could find his way through such a place. It soon
became apparent, however, that Abdul had a definite
plan, for he seemed systematically to search out certain

booths. His direction never faltered. He knew the market intimately.

Somewhere in the middle of the bazaar we stopped at a small table at the junction of a street and an alley. Abdul started a conversation with a man partially hidden behind a gray robe. He had lamps and vases and small bits of jewelry for sale, like many of the others we had seen.

It seemed that the man knew something about the jeweled piece. He spent some time passing the wing back and forth in his hands, pointing out various details. Abdul would say something in Arabic and the man would grunt or nod in recognition. After a brief pause Abdul reached into his pocket and carefully placed a stack of coins on the vendor's table. These he arranged in five neat rows.

There was a short animated conversation. Then Abdul did a surprising thing. He reached forward and withdrew one of the stacks of coins. The Egyptian's eyes opened wide in disbelief.

They entered into another feverish conversation, this time with much hand-waving and gesturing. The man paused. Abdul shrugged. Reaching forward he withdrew another stack of coins. Where there had once been five neat rows there were only three. The vendor looked as though he were going to cry. He raised his hands to his head and began jabbering in a loud, excited fashion. Abdul thanked him and returned one of the stacks of coins. The man grinned broadly. They shook hands and seemed to part the best of friends.

Much to my relief we moved quickly out of the bazaar. Apparently the vendor remembered a beggar who had come through a week before. He was an old man and he had tried to sell a jeweled wing similar to the one Abdul had carried.

Most of the jewelers had become suspicious because he wanted so much money for it. There was no way they could verify that it was real. In fact the vendor had at first thought that we were from the police and were trying to track down a forgery. When he saw the money being withdrawn, the temptation became too great and he told the entire story. The vendor was sure the man had come from Luxor or somewhere in the south. He had used the name "Muhammad." Here Abdul smiled, for nearly everyone in Egypt had Muhammad somewhere in his name.

This was all that the vendor admitted knowing. Later I asked Abdul how he came upon his unique system of bargaining. He smiled wryly and replied that there was an old Egyptian saying: "The pain of the blade is always greatest on feeling it withdrawn."

That evening at our usual tea Abdul told the professor what we had found. Reilly wondered if a trip to Luxor was called for. Abdul nodded. The professor could pose as a wealthy Englishman looking for artifacts and burial jewels. We could take one of the museum men with us to look at the offerings and help authenticate anything of real value. Once in Luxor Adbul could pass the word that the Englishman had much money and was willing to pay premium prices for authentic pieces.

Professor Reilly was not sure that such a disguise would work, but they both agreed that the temptation to a grave robber would be hard to resist.

"It would take me about three days to get ready," Reilly said. His eyes flashed with excitement.

That we would get a chance to travel up the Nile to the interior was extremely exciting news. Luxor was only a few miles from the fabulous Valley of the Kings, which had played so great a role in Egyptian archaeology.

On Sunday we took the evening train to Luxor, arriving early Monday morning. The professor had arranged for us to stay in a hotel just across from the ruins of one of the most famous temples of the New Kingdom. After we unpacked I spent an hour exploring the city. Abdul had already left by the time I returned, and the professor was busy writing letters. That afternoon Reilly invited me to accompany him to the Valley of the Kings.

What a hot and desolate place it is! No blade of grass, not a single plant grows anywhere. The entire valley is composed of gravel and stone resting like the crumbled ashes of some charcoal furnace between huge limestone cliffs. A guide reported that there had been no rain for 145 years.

Sixty-four tombs had been discovered in the area, all with the same general plan. A set of steps led down to a long corridor, which in turn ended in a burial chamber. The walls were magnificently decorated with various scenes and hieroglyphics. Except in the case of the tomb of Tutankhamen all statues and funeral ornaments had been stolen.

To see this godforsaken pit of dry and charred rock with mounds of gravel heaped across it made the task of looking for a new tomb seem impossible. The perseverance of Howard Carter, who had dug unsuccessfully in the valley for six seasons, was remarkable. Carter later recounted that on two occasions he had come within one yard of the single step which led downward to the tomb of Tutankhamen and yet had missed it. Incredibly, in 1922, in his last season and in the last area which he planned to search, he found the tomb on practically the first pitch of the shovel.

But that is the way of archaeology. Luck, perseverance, guesswork. How many hundreds of men had followed vague dreams, spent thousands of dollars, searched diligently for years to no avail? Even worse were the stories of the discovery of a tomb, the great hopes at finding the burial intact, and then the bitter disappointment that it had already been sacked by grave robbers centuries before. The yield had been small, the hours and toil colossal.

That evening we gathered for dinner at the Luxor Hotel. Abdul had not yet returned, but midway through the meal he appeared at the doorway covered from head to toe with dust. He refused to walk inside the dining room, but waved to us that he had had good luck. From the size of the turnout that began to drift into town searching for the professor the following day, he must have covered every village for a dozen miles around.

For the next four days Professor Reilly set up a small table and canvas chairs beneath the large columns in the ruins of a Luxor temple. Here, accompanied by Abdul and the museum representative, he received callers twice a day, once in the late morning and again in the evening shortly after tea. From the first afternoon on lines of Arab fellahin came to the ruins and waited patiently. The professor thanked each one politely, wrote down the objects offered, and cataloged them in a ledger. Each day he spent perhaps twenty or thirty pounds. By purchasing a smattering of everything he was able to maintain his guise without revealing that he was looking for a specific piece. In this way he hoped that the fellahin would continue bringing more of their findings.

At night, after dinner, we would sit in the professor's room and sift through the purchases of the day. Some of the alabaster vases and carved figurines looked incredibly old, but the museum representative assured me that most of them had been made during the past several months. The amount of forgery that we uncovered was staggering.

Obviously the entire business provided good income for the local villagers. One unique method of "antiquing" a small piece of jewelry was to feed it to a turkey. A day's journey through the digestive tract of one of these birds made it appear centuries old. The methods of the more clever forgers knew no bounds.

Unfortunately out of the hundreds of objects only two or three appeared to be of real archaeological value. By the fifth day nothing resembling the winged scarab had shown up, and we had begun to feel that the trip was a lost cause. The museum representative returned to Cairo and we were faced with spending the weekend in Luxor before returning ourselves.

Throughout the week I was in the habit of strolling down to the river to watch the boats at dusk. It was an extremely peaceful time of the evening and the view offered was certainly beautiful. During one of these

walks I looked around and saw a robed figure following me. Remembering my unpleasant experience in
Cairo I hurried forward, occasionally glancing over
my shoulder. If I speeded up, so did my pursuer; if I
slowed down, so did he. My first thought was to make
a wide circle and change direction so that I could
return safely to the hotel, but it soon became apparent that he was by himself. I decided to hide behind a
large grove of palms next to a walkway by the river.

The soft, padding footsteps came quickly. As he
passed, I stepped out and stood my ground. I was not
sure I could communicate with him, but I wanted to
let him know my displeasure at being followed.

"What do you want?" I cried.

For an instant, as he turned to face me, I had the
terrible feeling that he was going to pull a knife. Then
he cowered and pulled his hands up over his face.

"Do not hit, sir. Please, do not hit," he exclaimed.

In the fading light I saw that he was a defenseless
old man. His face was partially hidden by his robe.
His eyes and cheeks were terribly wrinkled. When he
spoke there were big gaps between his teeth. Those
few teeth remaining were yellow and in a horrible
state of decay.

"Oh, thank you, thank you," he said when he realized I was not going to strike him. He moved forward
and, assuming the position of a supplicant, bowed and
tugged lightly on my arm. "You are with the rich
Englishman?" he asked. Without waiting for an answer he led me toward a path by the river. "Come,
sir, I fear that I am being followed."

I walked with him down the pathway. Every few
steps he turned nervously and looked behind us or
craned his neck in either direction. After a few minutes I began to be jittery myself, even though I was
not sure what he was afraid of.

We arrived at a little corner in the pathway that
was sheltered by some palms.

"Praise Allah," he said. "I think we can talk here."
He paused and wiped his brow with an arm that was
crippled and bent.

"You are with the Englishman, no?" he asked again.

"That's right," I nodded impatiently.

"I have brought something he might want to see."

It occurred to me that he had undoubtedly seen me with the professor, and probably thought he could dupe me with some trifling artifact that he made.

"No money," I said angrily. After pulling my pockets out so that he could see the white insides, I turned and began walking away.

He caught me and tugged on my arm. "No, wait! Look what I have!" He reached inside his robe with his crippled arm and pulled out a small object wrapped in a dusty rag. It was the missing wing! The colors were identical. There was the same fine gold inlay along the stones. Everything seemed to match.

Far across the river an oar banged against a boat. The sound startled the old man, who instantly reached forward and grabbed the object from my hand. Hurriedly rewrapping it he pushed it back beneath his robe.

"How much?" he asked.

I had no money, but I wanted desperately to get him back to the professor so that he could examine the piece.

"Come to the Luxor Hotel. Meet me in the lobby; I will bring money."

"How much?" he asked again.

"I do not know," I shrugged. "The Englishman will tell you."

He thought this over, then smiled his wide and toothless grin. "By Allah, that's good," he said. "I, Muhammad, will come tonight."

He held out his hand, giving me only the tips of his fingers to shake. Quickly he limped down the path along the river, glancing furtively over his shoulder as he disappeared.

Eager to bring the news to the professor I jogged back to the hotel. As I reached the doorway I passed a group of four or five men, dressed in desert robes, crouching alongside the road and eyeing me suspiciously. I had never seen them before and something about them made me uneasy.

The professor was in the shower when I burst into his room. I waited patiently for a few minutes, then yelled to him that I had exciting news. He came out quickly, wrapping himself in a robe. After I explained what had happened, he wanted to know every detail about the old man, and he asked many questions about the jeweled wing. I could not remember whether the red stone had been above the blue or how many layers of stone feathers there were or if it looked as if it had a natural point of connection to the scarab. In exasperation I finally said that it had looked the same. It was only my judgment; the light had been poor. Perhaps I had made a mistake.

"Don't worry," the professor said when he saw my discomfort. "If the old man shows up tonight, we shall see soon enough."

We decided that I should post myself in the lobby for the remainder of the evening. The professor would take dinner with Abdul and retire to his room. On the first sight of our expected visitor I would bring him immediately upstairs.

I went down to the lobby and spent the better part of the evening pacing back and forth, wondering if old Muhammad had really understood. Several hours passed. I became increasingly fretful until, just before ten o'clock, a hunched figure suddenly darted into the lobby. It was Muhammad. He greeted me with that peculiar handshake, using only the tips of his fingers. I explained to him that the "rich Englishman" was upstairs. He nodded enthusiastically and followed me into the elevator.

When we reached the professor's room, the sight of Abdul made him nervous again. Abdul explained in Arabic that he worked for the Englishman. He invited him to sit down, but the old man refused.

In the fashion which I was now becoming accustomed to, they spent the next half hour chatting about the weather, the town, and the coming season of floods, making no reference to the jeweled wing. These introductory periods served as a way of sizing up one's opponent, and the more important the reason for meeting, the longer the prelude of idle discussion.

When the small talk ebbed, the professor asked if the old man had something for him to see.

As he had done earlier in the evening, the Arab placed his crippled hand underneath the robe and produced the piece of cloth. Once the object was uncovered, he laid it upon a table beneath a light so that it was in full view. It was truly a beautiful piece of craftsmanship, and the red and blue stones glistened brightly. Surely this was the missing wing.

Professor Reilly examined it for a long time before he passed it over for Abdul to scrutinize. But the frown on the professor's face indicated that all was not well.

"How much, sir? Thank you," Muhammad asked.

The professor shook his head.

The old man did not understand and repeated the question.

"I am sorry," the professor said slowly. "This is not the real thing. It is a clever imitation."

My heart sank. I had brought the professor a forgery!

I started to mutter an apology, but the professor held up his hand.

"No deal," he said.

The Arab uttered a string of oaths and protested violently. As his voice rose, Abdul talked to him firmly. Soon a shouting contest arose. Finally the professor stood up and calmed him. After pacing back and forth for a few minutes the old man seemed to see that he was getting no place. With a violent movement, he grabbed the forgery and placed it back in the cloth, then stuffed it into the resting place beneath his robe. I thought that he would go and that would be the end of it.

Instead he produced another rag and unraveled it in front of our eyes. In retrospect I think that he probably showed me the original down by the river, then substituted his own clever forgery in hopes of pawning it off on the professor.

The instant the second package was opened the difference was obvious. There was a definite luster about this second piece which had not been present in the first. The stones were thinner, almost transparent when held up to the light. The gold inlay was much more delicate. The professor's eyes widened. He looked at the wing closely, turning it over in his hand. A broad grin crossed his face.

"Bravo!" he said underneath his breath.

"How much, sir, how much?" Muhammad asked.

Reilly went into the back room and came out with the two other pieces of the winged scarab. Placing them upon the table he arranged the pieces so that the two wings fit perfectly into the sides of the scarab. It was a truly beautiful piece of jewelry and, with all three pieces joined, it looked to be of immense worth. Twenty, thirty, maybe fifty thousand pounds.

The old man's mouth slowly fell open. For the first time he realized that we were far more than a "rich Englishman" and some naive friends. Suddenly he darted forward and grabbed his jeweled wing. Clutching it in his trembling hand, he backed away from the table.

"Abdul, tell him that the wing alone is useless to us," Reilly said. "It is the burial place that we are concerned about. If he wants a hundred pounds I will give it to him, if he will show us where he found these pieces. Remind him that entering the royal tombs is a crime and that he might have charges brought against him for possession and attempts to sell this jeweled wing. It is not his to sell. It belongs to the Egyptian government."

As Abdul translated, a cloud drifted heavily across Muhammad's face.

"No, no," he exclaimed. "A trick! It has been a trick!"

He turned his back to us and marched across the room. As he reached the far wall, he uttered an oath and threw the jeweled wing at the professor. It was not a good throw. It flew across the room and smashed into the side of the wall, breaking into a hundred pieces. In the same instant he wrenched open the door and was gone.

For a moment we were frozen. The sight of this priceless piece of jewelry dashed to pieces on the floor was too much for us. The professor erupted from his chair.

"Get him!" he cried.

Being the closest to the door I turned and leaped after him. For a crippled old man he moved with amazing speed. We were on the third floor. By the time I had raced into the hallway I could hear him pounding down the stairs. As I reached the lobby, his dark and tattered form was lunging into the night. I ran out of the hotel after him, but it was no use. In the dark there was no means of pursuit.

I walked slowly back to the room, disappointed and empty inside. We had found the missing wing, but now it was dashed to pieces. And the man who knew the location of the tomb, if there was one, was gone.

Professor Reilly was crouched on the floor, gathering up the broken pieces. Incredibly enough he was laughing.

"A very clever fellow," he chuckled. "Remind me never to underestimate the Egyptian fellah."

I felt angry. I could not understand anything amusing about the incident. A priceless object had been broken beyond repair.

"It was the forgery." The professor laughed. "Look at the stones. They are not the same. Somehow he switched the pieces when he had his back turned and threw the forgery against the wall."

I looked at Abdul and we both began laughing. The old man had outwitted us. At the last minute he had pulled a sleight of hand which had fooled us completely.

"Well, what do we do?" I asked.

The professor shrugged. "I guess we wait. Tomorrow Abdul can try to locate him in one of the villages. Perhaps he'll reconsider and come back. We must make sure that word gets around we are not with the police. I think that is what scared him."

The next morning at breakfast Abdul gave us devastating news. The old man had been found near the hotel, murdered. The jeweled wing had disappeared; and it looked as if our last hopes of finding the burial place were gone.

6

WE LINGERED at the hotel for the rest of the day hoping for further information. Old Muhammad may have been able to fool us, but he had not been so lucky with his countrymen. Abdul had noted a group of Arabs lurking around the hotel. In fact it may have been the same devilish lot that I had seen the previous evening as I hurried back from the river to bring the professor the news. Whatever role they might have played in the events was unknown.

Perhaps their suspicions were aroused when they saw the old man entering the hotel. When he came running out after our confrontation they may have followed him. His crippled body had been found dumped in an irrigation ditch. His neck had been severed, and a deep wound penetrated his abdomen.

We spent the day sadly, trying to think of some suitable plan. After dinner Reilly decided that we should return to Cairo. We could wait in Luxor for another month with no results. It was unlikely that the thieves would try to barter with the professor, and we knew that they had no idea of the burial location.

I retired early. The professor and I had adjacent rooms and I could hear him shuffling around as he packed. I was in bed reading when suddenly there was a violent knocking at the door. It was so loud that I thought it was my own door, and I sprang from bed to open it. In the hallway a young, dark-skinned Arab was standing in front of the professor's room. He was dressed in the simplest street clothes and was not much older than I. As he beat loudly on the door, he called out in Arabic. The professor opened his door and, on seeing me in the hall, motioned for me to fetch Abdul.

Abdul and I followed the young man inside. The professor asked him if he wanted to sit, but he shook his head, preferring to stand. As he spoke, Abdul translated.

He apologized for interrupting us at night. He knew that we were busy people and he would not bother us with anything of small importance. His life was in danger and so were the lives of his family. His father had been murdered the night before. Ever since his death people had come to his village asking about a winged scarab. It was the curse of the pharaohs, he said, and he knew it would bring no good. He had warned his father about it.

We were back on the right track again.

When he was a child, Abdul translated, fifteen, twenty years before, his father had taken a three-day trip up the Nile to visit relatives who lived some distance to the south. He had made the journey with two friends. On the way back they had camped during the night. Somehow one of their camels had broken free. As they searched for it in the morning they came upon a strange find, the ruins of an old city, or a temple, buried in the sand. They found the camel in the shade of a tall cliff. While trying to coax it back his father noted a passageway leading into the cliff. Fearing discovery by his friends his father had not stopped, but instead he returned several months later with his son. Inside the cave they found many things which were very old, a few of which his father collected and brought back to the village. They never told anyone else about the cave, and over the past several years his father had sold some of the pieces one by one. With time some of the people of the village had become suspicious, so his father decided to go to Cairo. Since then they had had nothing but bad luck. One of his sisters had become ill. They discovered that their crops had been infected with some kind of blight. And now his father had been killed. He was afraid that harm might come to his mother and the rest of the family. He did not care about the treasure of the cliffs. He would give it all away.

Here the young Egyptian broke down and began to cry. It had been a terrible ordeal.

The professor interrupted and assured him that it was best to turn everything over to the government. They could arrange for his protection. Once the treasure was safe he would have nothing to worry about. The professor added that the young man was very brave to come to him and he appreciated the gravity of his situation. When he asked the young man if he could take us to the site that his father had discovered, the Egyptian nodded. It was a full day's travel from Luxor. He had been there only once, but he thought he could find it again.

The young man seemed extremely grateful, shaking all of our hands and bowing several times. Reilly asked Abdul to express to him the urgency of traveling to the site as soon as possible.

I had envisioned a jeep or land rover. But the Egyptian replied that there were no roads. We would have to go in a small caravan.

"Camel?" the professor asked.

Abdul nodded.

"And how do we arrange it?"

Abdul conversed with the Egyptian for some minutes before turning toward us. "There is a small stable on the outskirts of town. We will probably need two men besides Muhammad to help us with the camels."

"Good," Reilly answered. "We will want a day to get food and some kind of tents, blankets, and cooking gear. Let's plan to leave the day after tomorrow. Have the young man meet us here."

"He wants to join us on the other side of the Nile at the ferry landing," Abdul translated.

"Just as good," the professor answered. "Ask him if there is anything he wants us to do for him or his family?"

The Egyptian thought about this for a minute, then declined. Shaking our hands again, he smiled bravely and departed.

Later that night I went to the lobby with a cable addressed to the museum representative who had accompanied us to Luxor.

MUHAMMAD ABD ALLAZAR
ASSISTANT CURATOR
MUSEUM OF ANTIQUITIES
CAIRO

SUSPECT WE MAY COME UPON NEW FIND SOUTH
OF LUXOR STOP FINAL NEWS IN THREE DAYS STOP
HOPE FOR THE BEST

J ARNOLD REILLY

When I returned the professor had opened his suitcase
and was cleaning a small black revolver. Seeing my
astonishment he smiled.

"Ever use one of these?" he said.

I shook my head. I had fired some of my father's
pistols as a boy, but I didn't even know how to load
them.

After a few minutes' instructions he handed me the
revolver and a small box of shells. "Keep these hidden in your clothes," he said. "In case something happens to me I'd feel better if both you and Abdul
carried some protection. There's no telling what we
are going to find."

7

THE FOLLOWING day was occupied by preparations for our departure. Abdul would arrange for the transportation, I was in charge of the blankets and tents, and the professor purchased the food. As usual Abdul was intimately involved in everything. The best blankets I could obtain were a half dozen wool ones from an Arab trader for three times their normal value. Abdul took one look at these and sent the man scurrying to the back room, where he found another half dozen of fine pure wool for only half the price. In like fashion he oversaw the procurement of three small tents and assisted the professor with the food. By the afternoon, with most of the work completed, he disappeared, saying he would make the final arrangements for transportation and meet us the next morning on the west bank of the Nile.

We left Tuesday at the crack of dawn. The first rays of light were creeping above the horizon as we crossed the Nile. By six in the morning many of the Egyptian fellahin were already well into their working day. Groups of them drove oxen and water buffalo down to the river to drink.

As we reached our landing, a caravan consisting of six camels and two donkeys was waiting patiently for us by the river. The camels were crouched on all fours. Sitting in front of them was a small group of men. One of them stood up as we approached. He was dressed in the headdress and white robe typical of the Sahara nomad. It was Abdul.

It took us an hour to pack and load all the gear. By this time we were joined by the young Egyptian who would act as our guide. Abdul introduced him as

Muhammad Rhamon el-moshen. Thereafter we called him Muhammad One, to distinguish him from our two camel drivers, who were also named Muhammad. He greeted us as long-lost friends and loaded his gear upon the backs of the camels. By seven o'clock, with the sun already burning into the harsh desert rock, we were ready to start.

At first we passed through a number of small villages. Women stopped work to watch us. Little children darted back into their houses, peeking out at us from the doorways. The sun rose higher still, moving above the great sandstone bluffs which mark the edges of the Sahara.

At the end of a valley we ascended a narrow pass before following a faint mountain trail for almost an hour. Finally we descended again and moved slowly along the broad base of the mountains. The terrain was desolate and bare. There was nothing living, nothing moving. Each part of the desert looked like every other. As the sun gradually rose higher, the perspiration flowed steadily down my neck. There was no respite, no comfort, no bit of shade. The soft colors of the desert were gone. Everywhere were shimmering waves of heat.

At eleven o'clock we stopped. Abdul dismounted. By his reckoning we were still four hours away. The camels were made to kneel, and we crouched in the sun while Abdul offered us some water, telling us to put it around our neck and under our arms.

Neither of our drivers seemed fatigued, nor did Muhammad One, who came and crouched down beside me and offered me some of his water. I was amazed at their stamina. Fortunately we had only a half day's travel ahead. Another two or three days and the professor and I couldn't have made it.

As we crouched beneath the burning sun, trying to find some faint breeze or inch of shade, one of the camel drivers came running back to say there was a disturbance behind us. In the distance a small line of dust rose from the base of the mountains. The professor took out a pair of binoculars and watched for some minutes but said he could not make anything out.

Abdul then tried the glasses and peered through them for a long time before putting them down.

"Probably a passing caravan going out into the desert. There is an oasis five days' travel from here."

Muhammad One, however, was not so easily convinced. He was worried that a band of villagers, or perhaps the same group of rogues that had killed his father, had followed us. Certainly our grand departure had not been secretive. But the professor disagreed. Someone following us all the way from Luxor was unlikely.

"There are occasional bands of robbers who live back in the hills," he said. "For that reason Muhammad One is right. We should at least be prepared."

I remembered the gun the professor had given me, which was tightly strapped upon the camel's back, hidden deep inside my clothes bag. It would not be of much use against a group of bandits swooping down upon us. Then Abdul did a surprising thing.

He casually produced a huge curved knife and patted it lightly on the blade. Muttering something in Arabic he slipped it back inside his robe and looked up as if nothing had happened. I had no idea that such a quiet and gentle man could be so casual about violence. But now, out here in the desert, I think I saw Abdul as he really was. He was originally of desert nomad stock. In his early years he had drifted away from his family, probably because of his greatly inquisitive mind. Once he had obtained an education, he found it impossible to return to the life of his people. So he had compromised, devoting his life to the study of ancient Egypt.

It was our good fortune that he had met the professor. Now, seeing him in his natural environment, his huge frame covered by a headdress and robes, I finally understood that mysterious element that I had suspected the first night I saw him. He did not really belong to our time, but to a day when great men such as he roamed the desert bringing treasure and harems and tents across the burning sands.

We rested until midafternoon. By then the dust

trail behind us was gone. Whoever it had belonged to had disappeared.

After an hour we turned directly toward the mountains, passing over a ridge before descending into a broad valley flanked by huge cliffs on either side. Here the professor called a halt and dismounted. He had seen something beside the path. Kicking away a pile of loose stones he uncovered a small boulder that had blended in perfectly with the rest of the terrain. Grunting Reilly pulled the rock until it stood upright. It appeared to be part of some kind of monument, perhaps the top of one of the tall painted stelae that one sees scattered through the old temples. Faintly etched on the surface of the stone were the traces of hieroglyphics which weather and time had all but obscured. We spent another five minutes wandering around the area but found no other carvings. Finally we mounted and continued on into the interior of the valley.

"Very strange," the professor said. "I don't recall ever hearing of any temples in this area."

Muhammad One now pointed to a peculiar outcropping of rocks on one side of the mountain.

"He thinks it is here," Abdul translated. "He reminds us that he has not been here for ten years, but he remembers the pointed rocks at the crest of the cliffs. They were what his father used as a guide."

We had reached the middle of the valley. We stopped again and the professor climbed a small rise to scan the area. Finally he shook his head. "If there is anything here it is buried by the desert," he said.

We rode toward the strange rocks on the crest of the mountain. The valley was at least a mile wide. As we crossed toward the cliffs, it became apparent that we were moving into a huge natural depression.

"Look," Abdul grunted. Stretched out before us along the valley floor were the faint remains of a temple. Because of the peculiar depression you could not possibly see it traveling through the middle of the valley. Even here the desert had hidden almost all of the ruins. They had been buried so thoroughly that there was only the barest suggestion of what might have existed before.

A fever of excitement rushed through us.

"Very close now," Abdul said. "Muhammad thinks we are very near."

Next to the cliffs were traces of more ruins. Broken pillars, the faint suggestion of stairs running toward the base of the cliff, one fractured arm which belonged to a statue buried somewhere in the sand. Nothing was left standing, yet it was obvious that a great structure had existed here. By pacing off the perimeter we were able to outline a huge platform that appeared to be a hundred yards across. A number of broken pillars lay scattered through the sand. At the base of one of these the professor brushed away the debris. A group of hieroglyphics came into view. He paused and gasped with amazement.

"Khufu!" he said in utter disbelief. Abdul rushed over to him. I followed in quick pursuit.

"It's the cartouche—the insignia—for Khufu!" *

Cartouches were characteristic insignias of various rulers, similar to signatures. Each king had his own set of hieroglyphics, always enclosed in an oval, and they

---

* Centuries before the translation of hieroglyphics the Greek historian Herodotus ascribed the Great Pyramid at Giza to the pharaoh Cheops, of the fourth dynasty, and it is this name which has been traditionally associated with the builder of the Great Pyramid. In recent years the cartouche for Khufu was found with quarry marks on some of the stone blocks inside the pyramid. We now know the correct Egyptian name for Cheops is "Khufu" Using the phonetic pronunciations of the hieroglyphics inside the cartouche, the symbols represent:

KH   U   F   U

Usually the cartouche is preceded by a curved plant and a bee, standing for the King of Upper and Lower Egypt.

were commonly inscribed upon a temple, or various statues or pillars to commemorate him.

The cartouche meant that the temple ruins were very old. It also meant that we had stumbled upon a previously undescribed find. Neither the professor nor Abdul had ever read of any temple ascribed to the Pharaoh Khufu in this area.

It was now six o'clock, and the professor called a halt. We decided to pitch camp on the floor of the platform. Despite my excitement I was completely fatigued. Wisely Reilly decided not to explore further but to settle down, get something to eat, and enjoy a good night's rest. We had the entire next day to search through the ruins.

Dinner that night consisted of dried meat, canned fruit, and several cups of water. I never thought anything so simple could taste so good. Then we all turned in. For a few moments I stared up at the clear Egyptian night wondering what great finds might be in store.

I wanted to dream of temples and strange jewels and ancient kingdoms of incredible wealth. Instead my thoughts kept returning to that damned camel. Every time I closed my eyes I was swaying back and forth on the poor creature's back, trying desperately to hold on. At least until morning I was doomed. Throughout the night my mind constantly plodded up one dune and down another, chasing some phantom oasis which always remained just one more mountain away.

8

WHEN I awoke, the sun was edging the eastern cliffs, casting a dim red glow into the valley. Our camel drivers were already attending to the camels and Abdul sat by a small fire preparing some tea. Muhammad One was walking at the base of the cliffs some distance away.

As the sun continued to rise, light flooded the valley with the force of a great surge of tide.

"Did you notice the crest of rocks Muhammad One used to guide us?" Abdul asked.

At the top of the cliffs the line of the mountains ran in a gently sloping contour until it reached the middle of the valley. At the approximate location of the temple an outcropping of rocks jutted abruptly above the cliffs and was visible far out into the desert.

"Remind you of anything?" Abdul asked.

Violet shadows streamed toward the valley floor. In the early morning light the crest of the rocks looked like a human head.

"Abdul, you're right!" the professor exclaimed. "I hadn't noticed."

The light was changing fast. With each moment the rocks seemed to outline more clearly the unmistakable shape of a face contoured in a broad head cloth. Two boulders struck out from the base of the figure like paws.

"The Sphinx!" I exclaimed.

Professor Reilly nodded. "Almost as if it had been carved," he said. In another instant the light had changed again and the figure was lost.

"It's very strange," the professor said. "The Great Sphinx is part of the complex of buildings with the

three pyramids of Giza. It was supposed to have been
built in the Old Kingdom in the fourth or fifth dynasty, around the time of the pyramid of Khufu. But
here? Out here in this desolate valley we find a
cartouche from Khufu, a temple half-buried in the
sand, and above it is this peculiar sphinxlike outcropping? I wonder . . ."

I wanted to ask him about his thoughts, but before
I could catch his attention Muhammad One joined us
on the platform, very excited and gesturing wildly.

"He thinks he has located the crevice," Abdul said.
"It's been so long since he was here that he was not
sure he could find it. He left early this morning. He
can take us there now."

The professor rubbed his hands together and
glanced at me.

"You ready, St. John?" He winked.

"Yes, sir," I answered. I could feel the excitement
hanging on his words.

We rolled our blankets, snuffed the fire, and the
professor unwrapped two high-powered battery lights
which he had brought especially for this occasion.
"Let's get moving," he said.

We followed Muhammad One down the embank-
ment toward the cliffs. Less than one hundred yards
from the platform was a pile of rubble which we had
to climb over. Mixed in with the rocks and sand were
broken pillars and pieces of temple stone. At the base
of the cliff was a half-hidden cave leading into the
rock, and the opening was so small it would barely ad-
mit the hunched figure of a man.

One by one we followed the professer inside the
crevice. The passage led to a sizable cave. The beam
of the lights searched out the perimeters. Thirty feet
back, twenty feet on either side, were solid rock
walls. But there was no evidence of carvings or burial
jewels. On the dusty floor we found some old cracked
vases, but nothing more.

Muhammad One wrung his hands.

"He is sure this is the cave," Abdul said. "When
he was here before he helped his father pull some of
the jewels out of a cache right here by this wall."

We looked again. Searching inch by inch we covered the entire floor, but whatever had been there was gone. The cave held nothing of value.

We crawled back out of the entrance, slapping the dust off our faces and arms. We were all terribly disappointed. Abdul spent some time reviewing Muhammad's story again, but it still held. The boy was sure this was where his father had brought him. If there had been anything, it was looted and long gone.

"We will need to notify the government," the professor said. "At least we have discovered the ruins of a temple and perhaps a small city, which must be of some historical significance. Someone will have to come in and excavate the area."

During the rest of the morning we carefully searched the base of the cliff, but there was no other entrance to be found. Muhammad One was horrified to have brought us all this way to no avail and continually apologized for his error. Our camel drivers were interested in our search and also seemed disappointed when we showed them the empty cave.

At noon we broke off our exploration and settled into the shade of the cliffs. I poured water down my front, trying to get some relief from the heat. It seemed to be 120 in the shade.

The professor walked over and sat down beside me. "You sleep well last night?" he said.

"A little sore from the ride," I answered, "but, everything considered, I did okay. Why?"

He looked around to be sure no one could hear what he was saying.

"Did you hear anything stirring around the camp?" I shook my head.

"Abdul said one of our drivers was gone last night for about an hour. He got up once and thought he saw a small light above the cliffs, flashing a signal down to the valley floor. It may have been a funny reflection from the moon, but I doubt it. He wouldn't make a mistake like that."

"What does that mean?"

"Abdul thinks we should be prepared for something funny," the professor answered. "When you get back to your clothes, slip your revolver out and carry it with you."

I nodded.

"We can talk about it after dinner," Reilly said.

We were surrounded by mountains on three sides. From some perch above us an observer could easily watch our activities. I glanced at our two camel drivers, who were squatting in the shade, leaning against a huge boulder. So far they had been both agreeable and cooperative. And Muhammad One, I was sure, was beyond reproach. Maybe everyone was just getting a little jumpy. If only Abdul had not been alarmed, I might have dismissed it all.

After the heat had begun to subside, we continued to explore the ruins. To one side of the temple had been a sizable complex of buildings. The professor scraped the sand away from the various pillars and recorded the hieroglyphics. He found the cartouche for Khufu two more times. Otherwise the afternoon passed without incident, and we settled into the evening meal shortly before sunset.

I was gnawing on a piece of dried bread when Muhammad One ran up to the professor and grabbed him by the arm. Pointing back to the cliffs he motioned excitedly for us to follow.

"He has seen something he wants to show us," Abdul said. Half-running, half-stumbling, we followed him toward the cliffs. At a little rise in the ground we stopped.

Droves of bats flew out of the side of the cliff. They came out of two places. One was quite high on the cliff and the second was the crevice we had entered that day. Thousands of them streamed out in a steady cloud.

"Bryan, bring me the lights!" the professor cried excitedly.

I sprinted across the rubble to the platform and found the two flashlights. I was not sure what was so important about the bats, nor why the professor was so concerned about getting the lights. When I returned to the crevice, the stream of bats had lessened considerably.

"Must be some type of a large cavern farther on," Reilly exclaimed. And then I remembered that we had seen no sign of bats or their droppings in the cave we'd searched.

We ducked and entered the crevice. For a moment the room was full of bats. They seemed to fly from every direction. Then, just as suddenly, they were gone. The lights revealed a narrow horizontal cleft in the side of the rock, perhaps twelve feet from the crevice floor. Above it was a second and then a third. Each slit was no more than six inches high.

"Could be ventilation shafts," the professor exclaimed. He motioned for me to step up on Abdul's shoulders. Grabbing a handhold in a crack I hoisted myself onto Abdul's back. He slowly lifted me up to the lowest of the slits.

As I pulled myself even with the opening a fresh, cool breeze struck my face. I shined a beam of light into the space beyond. It fell off into nothingness. I angled it downward. The beam shone upon a neat and polished floor which gradually descended into the heart of the cliff. Forcing the light as far into the opening as I could I tried to discover the dimensions of the space. I shined the light up and then to the right. Suddenly, burning out of the darkness, was a sight I will never forget. Staring out from the dark mysterious space were two huge, luminous eyes.

"I see . . . two . . . two eyes," I gasped.

"What?" the professor exclaimed.

Gradually, as I squinted into the darkness, I saw a face with a long billed nose like no animal I had ever seen. Then I realized that it was a statue. Strange reflecting disks had been used for the eyes. I ran the light to the right and left and discovered more statues on either side. They were huge, at least twenty feet tall, dominating the room by their massiveness.

We stumbled out of the crevice a half hour later, stunned by our findings. There was evidently a passageway at the base of the cliffs which led into the heart of the mountain, a passageway so cleverly concealed that our best efforts had not uncovered it. If it had not been for the bats, we would not have been aware of it at all.

The sun had gone down now and it was quite dark. Back at the platform our camel drivers had built a fire. We crowded around it and tried to gather our thoughts.

"There has to be some way inside," the professor said. We had covered every inch of the cliff. The question now was whether we should try to stay one more day on limited provisions or return with a bigger crew. Our answer was unanimous. No one felt that we could give up now.

It was a beautiful night. The air was warm and I lay for a long time staring up at the stars. When I rolled over, only Abdul seemed awake, his eyes shining in the light from the fire. A jackal called in the distance. Above us the stars looked close enough to touch. I stood up and went over to the fire. In a moment Abdul was crouched next to me. We both sat silently staring into the flames.

"What do you think we'll find?" I whispered.

He thought for a moment without answering. "I am not sure," he said. "The professor thinks that the father of Muhammad, the old man with the jeweled wing, must have broken into the main chamber itself and somehow brought some of the things out. Perhaps he used the crevice as a storage area. Maybe it is all empty. I cannot tell."

Trying to hide my own eagerness I asked about the statues. "But the gods of the underworld? Aren't they always found inside tombs?"

"Sometimes," Abdul answered. "Maybe it is different here."

He would not commit himself any further. He seemed to be in a strange mood, and I felt I was intruding. Finally excusing myself I went back to bed. I turned from time to time and saw him hunched over the embers of the fire.

I awoke before dawn. I was not sure why or how, but I awoke instantly and I had the immediate feeling that something was very wrong. I lay absolutely still and listened. I heard the faintest clink of footsteps, as if someone were walking quietly on stone. I turned very slowly in my blanket. The moon had gone down. The fire was out. Everything was pitch black beneath the stars. I could make out the faint shapes of Abdul and the professor in their blankets. Then a hideous shriek carried across the desert and echoed off the cliffs.

Instantly all of us were on our feet. I groped desperately for my revolver. The professor flashed on his light.

In the open sound is a deceptive thing. Even though I had been awake, I was not sure exactly where the scream had come from.

Suddenly we heard the scuffling sound of someone scrambling on the rocks, the sound small pebbles make when loosened underfoot. Then there was nothing. We listened carefully. Five minutes passed and still we heard nothing.

"Everything all right?" the professor whispered.

"Yes," I answered. The professor flashed his light across the two Arabs. One of them had drawn a knife and was poised, ready to lunge at anything that came near. Below us the camels were shuffling and grunting nervously on their tethers.

"Everyone here?" the professor asked.

"Muhammad!" Abdul cried. Our youthful guide was gone. We listened quietly for another five minutes, but the awful cry did not leave us with much hope. I feared that Muhammad One had come to the same terrible end as his father.

Another half hour passed, and finally we started the fire. Until daylight there was nothing left for us to do.

9

WITH THE first rays of light we spread out across the ruins looking for some trace of Muhammed One, but he had vanished with no more trace than the wild cry we had heard in the night.

When we met back at the platform, the professor was concerned about our finding our way to Luxor. Abdul assured him that he had watched the landmarks carefully and that he would be able to guide us back. Reilly decided that we would continue with our plan of staying the additional day. Besides, he reasoned, our young guide might not be dead but merely injured and able to work his way back to our camp.

The one advantage of rising early in our search for Muhammad was another chance to observe the bats. For the first fifteen or twenty minutes of daylight great clouds of them swooped down from the sky and disappeared into the cliffs, primarily through the second hole high in the face of the rocks. This opening was perhaps thirty feet above the ground in a narrow cleft not far from the crevice we had explored.

This second opening was as big as a man's body, and although the rock was smooth, there were several rough edges along the cliff which offered handholds for someone agile enough to climb. I volunteered, but the professor thought it would be better to let one of our camel drivers give it a try.

When offered the job of scaling the cliff with a rope on one arm and a light in the other, they both vigorously refused. They were very superstitious, and the disappearance of Muhammad One did not help. They protested violently that the curse of the pharaoh would be upon anyone who entered the cave. The bats, they said, were an ominous sign in themselves.

I volunteered again, but the professor refused. I argued that I was sure I could make it up the cliff. Just as I was beginning to make some headway, Abdul interrupted saying that we could bargain with one of the Arabs. As usual money was able to overcome the strongest superstition, but five Egyptian pounds seemed outrageously expensive for a relatively small feat. As it turned out, however, I would be extremely glad that I did not go. Were it not for the fact that the Arabs' greed was stronger than my own stupidity, I do not think I would have left that desolate valley alive.

In a few minutes we rigged up one of our camel drivers with the rope and light, and he began to scale the cliff. He clambered up the rocks like a monkey, and when he reached the opening in the cliff he tossed us the rope, throwing the other end into the hole. He peeked his head in first and shone the light ahead. In a second he popped back out, saying that he could see the floor of the cavern less than thirty feet below. Abdul tied the free end of the rope to a rock, and the camel driver descended into the cavern.

He had not been gone for more than half a minute when the most awful cry erupted from inside the cliff. I leaped up on the cliff wall and swung over the rocks hand-by-hand until I had reached the top of the crevice. Peering fearfully into the hole I could see nothing. The rope disappeared into a black void. Somewhere far off in a tunnel someone was running wildly. Scream after pitiful scream echoed down the hallway and made my hair stand on end. Finally there was one long wail and then all was silent.

This last yell produced a strange effect. Even though I was crouched at the top of the crevice peering inside, the sound seemed to erupt from the valley floor behind me. Both Abdul and the professor noticed this, too. For them it was much louder than the previous yells which had been muffled inside the cavern.

"There's a second opening!" the professor cried. It was now apparent that an underground passageway led from the temple directly into the chamber inside the rock. Somewhere in the ruins at the base of the temple was another entrance. It was here that we had heard the last scream of our camel driver.

We left the rope in place and rushed to the pile of rubble. Going over the ground inch by inch we came upon a depression which we hadn't noticed before. A broken pillar half-obscured a hole. By moving two rocks we were able to enlarge the opening. Cool air poured out of it. We had at last found the main shaft of the chamber.

Armed with our revolvers and Abdul's huge scimitarlike blade we carefully descended into the passage. The remaining camel driver refused to stay by himself and followed us inside.

Abdul led the way. A tunnel about seven feet high and four feet wide sloped gently downward. The walls were smooth and the floor had a polished luster, as if it had been laid from the finest stone. We had gone perhaps fifty feet in the direction of the cliffs when the flashlight beam caught something white in the distance.

It was the slumped figure of our Arab driver, a large gash across his left eye. He still held the light in his hand, but the glass and the bulb were smashed.

The professor leaned over him and felt for a pulse. "Dead," he said flatly.

There was a terrible grimace on the man's face. His eyes were wide and his lips drawn back. The skin began to prickle on the nape of my neck. What was down here in the bottom of the shaft? I felt for the comfort of my revolver. The remaining Arab, visibly trembling, refused to come near his dead companion.

It was then that the professor's systematic training paid off. "Let's get him undressed," he said. At first I could not understand what this would accomplish. We pulled off his robe and laid his naked body upon it. Reilly went over him carefully, the entire procedure taking less than three minutes.

"Ha!" he said finally. "That's our answer." He pointed out a large bluish area probably three inches

across on the man's left calf. In the center were two
small puncture marks. "Snake," he said.

"Cobra," Abdul nodded.

We pieced together the story. Shortly after the man
descended into the tunnel, the snake must have bitten
him from behind. Swinging at the reptile he knocked
out the light. Realizing that he would die, he had run
blindly down the corridor, screaming out his last
breath.

"Keep a sharp eye," the professor exclaimed.
"Don't put your hand anywhere you cannot see."

We pulled the body out of the way and covered it
with the robes.

"We'll have to come back and bury him," Reilly
said.

We grouped together and in single file followed
Abdul further into the depths of the passage. The corridor continued for another hundred feet before it
came to a flat, open chamber which widened to twenty
feet. Here a number of hieroglyphics were cut into the
rock. "Khufu again!" Reilly murmured. He pointed
out a small cartouche.

Along the walls were beautiful hieroglyphic paintings. There were pictures of strange beast-headed
men, and long snakes with legs, and drawings of boats
and various scenes of banquets and hunts, all bril-
liantly colored. At the end of this corridor was the
huge hall I had seen from the ventilation shaft the
evening before.

A beam of sunlight came down through an opening
high above the chamber, throwing a faint light upon
the faces of the statues. Carved out of the rock were
six massive figures seated in a semicircle. At the middle Osiris, with strange glowing eyes, presided over
the room like a judge. Each statue had the head of an
animal and the body of a man: Horus, the falcon-
headed god; Sobek, with the head of a crocodile;
Thoth, with an ibis bill; Seth, with the head of a don-
key; and Anubis, the jackal god.

The ceiling sloped upward in a curved dome. Here
golden hieroglyphics were painted on a deep-blue

background, signifying the eternal Egyptian night. Above the shoulders of the end statues two roughly hewn shafts led into the mountain. From the occasional fluttering we could tell that this was where the bats were sleeping. The builders of the hall must have cut these clefts for further ventilation; there was no other explanation for them.

Small torches were fixed to stone holders on each side of the entrance. Abdul produced a match and lighted one. To my surprise it still burned. After he lighted the other, the chamber was filled with weird, flickering light.

I wandered over to one side of the hall as the professor and Abdul were searching along the foot of one of the statues. During this time our remaining camel driver huddled at the back of the hallway, apparently fearing to proceed further. As I was admiring the statues, I glanced at my hand. I had reached forward to feel the carved surface of one of the statue's arms. There, coiled in the statue's lap, was a snake, wrapped in a tight coil, the exact position from which it could spring. I was less than a foot away. I froze in terror. The slightest motion might cause it to strike. A minute went by as sweat oozed out upon my brow. My heart throbbed in my chest. If the snake struck, I would catch the full force of it on my uncovered arm. Even my face was close enough to be a target. We had no antivenom. The crude snakebite kit which the professor carried was wrapped in his clothes at the campsite.

"Bryan, look at this," the professor said. I could just make him out from the corner of my eye. He was crouched across the room studying some pieces of writing.

"Bryan?"

It suddenly occurred to me that their motion, even from across the room, might cause the snake to strike. I dared not speak.

I could hear Abdul stand up. He must have seen my frozen state and instantly realized my predicament. He crept stealthily across the room. As he reached my shoulder his arm rose slowly behind me. A flashlight beam illuminated the snake. An instant later a blade of steel came crashing down. The head of the snake bounced off the rock and landed practically against my chest.

The professor laughed. Abdul was holding the coiled body of the snake in his hand. As he squeezed, it fell into powder. It was mummified. It had died centuries ago but had remained perfectly preserved by the desert heat.

Someone later told me that the fangs of the snake might still have carried dried poison, but that didn't matter. My whole life had already passed before me in those sixty seconds.

The professor blamed himself for not having searched the corridor more carefully, and we spent the next thirty minutes reexamining every inch of the hall. We discovered several small holes in the walls of the tunnel which might have offered escape routes, but there was no evidence of the cobra which had killed our camel driver.

We now began to search for an extension of the passage leading into the mountain. The presence of the mythological figures made the professor suspect we had come upon a tomb—a body would be judged by these gods before its passage into eternity. Everything pointed to this chamber as only one part of an elaborate burial complex. But where was the tomb?

Early Egyptian architecture is symmetrical and very well ordered—everything has a place, every structure is intricately linked to every other. It made sense that the tomb, if there was one, should have a close connection with the statue of Osiris, the chief deity who presided over the room. But how?

Using the palm of his hand, Abdul scraped away at the stone beneath the central figure of Osiris. A thick layer of dust had obscured the flat space between the legs. Suddenly he came upon a small hieroglyphic seal.

"The jackal and nine slaves!" Reilly cried. "It is a tomb! This is the mortuary seal."

With great excitement we rubbed at the stone until we had completely cleaned its surface. The slab was roughly four feet wide. In each corner was the small stamped seal. Yet there was nothing more than the huge stone slab.

"Possibly a granite plug," the professor said disappointedly. "It would take us months to move it."

As we backed away, Abdul let out an exclamation and bent forward. "A door!" Shining the light along the floor he pointed to faint markings on the stone. We pushed once but were unable to budge it. When we tried again, the stone began to move. We pushed harder until the stone gave way, swinging inward. Behind was a hole large enough for a man. The corridor was filled with scattered rock. In thirty minutes we had cleared the debris and proceeded down the passage. The corridor was small, perhaps three and a half feet in height. We crawled down it one by one. Again the air was fresh. The Egyptians had obviously taken great care to ensure the proper ventilation for the tomb.

We descended another hundred feet into the heart of the mountain, until the passage opened into a small chamber where we could stand. A further tunnel led forward for another twenty feet before it divided into three short corridors.

The first of these ended in a chamber which had once been sealed. The plaster was broken and the room itself was piled with junk: old baskets, a chair, some alabaster vases, and one small statue. We were extremely disappointed. It was the same old story. Sometime in the far distant past someone had entered the tomb and removed most of the valuables.

When we moved back to the central corridor and explored the second room, our spirits soared. As soon as we entered the room, the light beam fell upon an open stone sarcophagus. Inside the sarcophagus was the partially wrapped body of a single mummy, from which a portion of the inner bandages across the chest had been torn. Someone had been there, obviously in search of jewels. Except for some crumbled rocks the rest of the room was empty.

The third chamber yielded nothing.

We spent the next hour going back over the three rooms. Except for the mummy there was little of interest. Whatever had been buried there was gone. A huge

frown hung on Reilly's face. Even Abdul became sol-
emn and subdued.

We crawled back through the small corridor into
the Hall of the Colossus. "Very, very discouraging,"
Reilly said. "I suppose we should not have expected
more. Tomb robbers stop at nothing. Perhaps old
Muhammad merely got the leftovers of the find. Who
knows what treasures were removed?"

Abdul stood silent, deep in thought. "It is almost as
if they used this chamber for a decoy," he said slowly.

"Certainly if you wanted to hide the burial you
would not have placed the tunnel where it was," I
volunteered. "The door is a perfect fit, but with a little
knowledge anyone could find it."

"Where then would you place the tomb?" the professor asked.

"We should look in the least likely place," Abdul
said. "The tunnel is too obvious."

As we spread out across the Great Hall, going back
over every inch of the chamber, I suddenly noticed
that the remaining Arab camel driver had vanished.
Abdul laughed when I mentioned his disappearance.
"Probably gone outside. I am sure he thought he was
going to come to some terrible death."

During our search I noticed that bats were still fluttering out of the clefts high up along the outer statue's
shoulders. "How about the ventilation shafts?" I suggested.

"Too obvious," Reilly answered.

"We must look for something well hidden, remote,
yet connected with this chamber."

"Opposite the statue of Osiris," I offered.

"Possibly," the professor said, a new note of excitement to his voice. He must have felt something un-
spoken from Abdul. He paced quickly across the
chamber.

"Next to the very door that enters the hall," he said
suddenly. "That might be the most unlikely spot."

The answer came so quickly and so unexpectedly
that even now I still find it hard to believe. When Professor Reilly walked out of the corridor through the
passage, the sound of his footsteps changed tone. We

noticed the change only because we suspected a chamber in this area.

In seconds we were on our knees, prying at the stone. The edges were so tightly fit that the blade of Abdul's knife could hardly scrape between them. Once the edges were cleared, however, it came away freely. With the professor and myself straining with our fingers we were able to get a grip on the stone. Then, with Abdul pulling upward with all of his huge frame, we budged the slab up off the floor. Lying on our stomachs we squinted through the narrow crack and shone the light into the empty space below.

An incredible scene glowed before our eyes. A narrow row of stairs descended into a large chamber. The entire room glittered with gold. There was no other color. It was as if we had shone a gold flashlight into the tomb and everything reflected the same brilliance. A large sarcophagus rested upon the floor. Priceless jewels were everywhere.

Speechless we stared into the tomb. Finally Professor Reilly stood up. We lifted the slab and it fell into place with a heavy thud. The tomb was resealed, and we were surrounded again by massive gray walls. The statues stared solemnly upon us. The transition was complete. We had looked into a room of light and wealth and beauty, and now it was abruptly gone, replaced by the drab, dull reflection of the massive stone walls.

It was a moment of incredible triumph, of historical discovery. At such a time other men might have descended into the tomb, but not the professor. We had found what we had come for. It would take weeks—perhaps months—to sift through the treasure and catalog the finds. We had no way to carry anything back. We knew we could trust each other. It was just as well that the Arab camel driver had not been there, for then we would have had to protect the find. As it was, we felt an intense bond of companionship.

We walked slowly up the corridor to the fallen pillar, crawled out of the tunnel, and stood in the warm desert evening watching the last rays of the sun bathe the sphinxlike rock in flame.

Suddenly, with shouts of joy and backslapping and handshaking, we hugged each other in exuberance. Tears were pouring down the professor's cheeks. I could feel moisture well up in my own eyes. And Abdul? All he could do was to shake his head and make a funny clucking noise. For the moment he had completely lost his voice.

10

WE BURIED the camel driver in a shallow grave next to the entrance of the corridor. We returned to camp long after dark. The four camels and the remaining camel driver were gone. We were able to corral the two donkeys, which had been turned loose and were wandering in the desert close to camp. But the camels presented a different problem. Reilly was afraid we might not be able to make it back. Abdul assured him that we could, but we would have to travel more carefully, stopping for longer periods of rest.

I was sure that the death of the Arab's companion and the inherent fear of the tomb had been too much for the camel driver. Most likely he had taken the camels and run.

We posted a guard that night. The professor decided to take the first watch, then Abdul, and finally myself. We sat by the fire for a long time discussing the tomb. The moon had risen over the northeast corner of the mountains, full and very bright, casting the valley in a coat of silver, which bathed the ruins in an unreal glow. By midnight I had fallen into a light and restless sleep, when I felt a gentle tap on my shoulder. The professor was standing over me. "You too sleepy to get up?"

I was already on my feet. "No, sir. Everything okay?"

He nodded. "Over the next month there will be hundreds of people poring over the ruins," he said. "Things will never be quite the same. Go down into the hall. I think with the moon at its fullest you shall see a grand display."

I rubbed the sleep from my eyes. I was worried

about stepping on one of the cobras, but the professor assured me that the cool air would force them into warm crevices. Abdul had already been to the hall and said it was a perfect night.

As we walked across the ruins, shadows played tricks upon my eyes. It was almost as if the ancient city were alive.

"Go on alone from here," the professor told me. "You can find your way into the cavern. I'll be back at the fire. Take your time. You'll never find it like this again."

I nodded and took his light. As soon as he disappeared, a hundred fears began to creep into my mind. I saw threatening shapes in every shadow, and strange figures drifted across the ruins.

As I entered the tunnel, it seemed as if I'd left my body and all the things I had ever known behind. I could hear nothing except the soft sound of my footsteps. When I came to the Great Hall of the statues, the sight exceeded everything else I had seen the entire summer. Moonrays from the open passage above illuminated the faces of the statues and brought the gods to life. The eyes of Osiris shone. The beak of Horus glowed, the teeth of Anubis seemed to suppress a growl. The faces, stern and cold, judged all who came before their gaze.

Suddenly a faint scuffling noise from the passage broke the silence. Voices could be heard in the distance. As the sound of footsteps grew closer, a faint light appeared. It flickered as if it were a torch, and then a flood of terror overcame me. The voices were speaking Arabic!

Remembering the two ventilation shafts where we had seen the bats, I leaped into the lap of the corner statue and pulled myself to its shoulders. Groping upward I found one of the shafts and wedged myself inside. Bats fluttered off the walls at my intrusion. My hands sank into soft guano. The tunnel was small and cramped, but by pushing sideways I was able to swing my head around so that I could see into the gallery.

Just as I did this, the light from a torch illuminated the hall. A group of seven Arabs burst into the room, led by our runaway camel driver. But where were Abdul and the professor?

The Arabs stood in the center of the hall, jabbering to each other. The camel driver pointed to the doorway beneath the legs of Osiris. They pushed on the stone and it swung open. One by one they entered the passage, their voices echoing down the tunnel. After a few minutes they reappeared and with heavy sticks began to pound along the walls.

To my horror I realized they were looking for another passage. Their instincts were much better than ours, for they had immediately suspected the existence of another chamber. Theirs was a simple but effective testing procedure. I was not sure whether they thought that the three open tombs were merely false passages or whether they systematically searched a tomb when they could find no jewels. It occurred to me that they might have noticed our excitement when we left the tunnel and realized we had come upon a find. Somewhere up in the mountains they had been watching us all the time.

At one point the wall rang with a hollow sound and they marked this with a stripe of ashes from their flare.

As I watched, my fears began to rise. If they continued in this fashion, they would soon discover the tomb beneath the floor. They were working quickly and methodically. But what was worse was my growing suspicion that Abdul and the professor had met foul play. They would certainly find the treasure soon, and I was sure they would kill me without hesitation.

One of the Arabs climbed up the statue opposite me and poked a torch into the other ventilation shaft. He worked down the other statues and slowly approached. There was nothing I could do. I was completely helpless. Once discovered I could not get out of the hole quickly enough, even to try to fight.

The light of the flame moved its way up the shoulder of the statue toward my ventilation shaft. I could hear someone climbing up the statue. The faint odor of an unwashed body drifted up. It was the smell of death to me.

Then someone struck a hollow note on the floor.

With much excitement the others rushed toward him.
The Arab who had been climbing the statue leaped
down to join them, and I breathed a long desperate
sigh of relief.

Pointing to the outlines of the slab one of them gave
an excited cry, and the others began to shout trium-
phantly. I knew that incredible treasure would dazzle
their eyes in another moment. Struggling heavily they
pulled at the floor.

Just as the stone began to move, from somewhere
out of the depths of the tunnel a weird sound started
in the form of a moan that rose in intensity. Part
groan, part cry, it stopped as suddenly as it had
started, leaving the tomb in complete silence. The
Arabs looked at one another, not quite believing what
they had heard.

At first they wanted to ignore it. A moment passed,
and when the sound did not come again, they returned
to their task of prying up the stone. Then the sound
began again. One of them got up and started off into
the ascending passage. They had all drawn their
knives. The sound had obviously been made by something alive. Yet there was a certain unearthliness about
it. Was the curse of the pharaohs real? Had some
strange phenomena existed here for centuries, waiting
for intrusion of grave robbers before it was unleashed?

The third time the sound arose, it whispered in a
strange language. The Arabs' eyes widened, and they
began to speak rapidly to one another, casting fright-
ened glances around the room.

Suddenly an agonizing cry arose from one of the
Arabs. His back arched in a grotesque curve. He tried
to maintain his balance as his eyes rolled upward and
blood gurgled from his mouth. Stumbling forward he
fell into a heap upon the floor and did not move.

The camel driver who had betrayed us stood in the
middle of the room, holding his torch above his head.
He started to say something when his voice rose in a
terrible scream. He staggered once, then pitched forward, dropping the torch upon the floor. At the same
moment the torch which the Arabs had fixed to one of

the sockets in the wall went out. Only the faint, flickering light from the torch on the floor remained.

This strange turn of events proved too much for them. After standing stiffly for an instant they broke into a frantic run. Yelling and shrieking they raced out of the room and up the passage.

The bat excrement oozed softly under my arms. The tomb was cold. It was as if the huge stone figures had pronounced judgment upon the Arabs and they had died. And now I began to fear for my own life, for surely I was not immune to the terrible fate of the others.

But what had happened? What kind of supernatural thing stalked these corridors? What strange fate had extinguished the life of these men?

The moon had gone down. Only faint starlight crept into the tomb. I felt safe inside the ventilation shaft. I would wait for morning and then try to make it out.

In a few minutes a light appeared far down the corridor. It was the Arabs, I thought, and all my fears started up again. Someone called my name.

"Bryan?"

I was afraid to answer.

The voice called out again. The light approached. It was Professor Reilly. I had never been so glad to see anyone in my life.

"Up here!" I shouted.

"Thank God you're all right!" he said. "I thought they had killed you."

"Are they gone?" I asked hesitatingly.

"Yes." He laughed. "Scattered to the four corners of the desert. I don't think they'll be back. Terrible scare for the poor chaps. Oh, my!" he said. He had discovered the first fallen Arab and bent over to check his pulse.

I scrambled out of the shaft and down the arms of the statue. The professor turned the dead man over. There was a huge stab wound in the man's back. We moved to examine our camel driver. The jeweled handle of a long scimitarlike blade was embedded to the hilt in the man's chest.

"Abdul!" I gasped.

"Yes," the professor nodded. "Apparently our driver was in cahoots with this lot the whole time. Muhammad One was right. We had been followed all the way from Luxor. The smell of treasure brings out the very worst in people."

"But how . . ." I said in amazement. "The loud noise, the strange cry . . ."

"Did you think it was the curse of the pharaohs?" Reilly smiled.

I threw up my hands. "I didn't know what to think —I was completely dumbfounded."

"Abdul found a side shaft running parallel to the main tunnel yesterday afternoon. He hadn't said anything about it, thinking it might come in handy, and as usual he was right. Shortly after you left for the hall, we saw a light out on the desert and figured they were coming. We snuck out into the desert. When they reached the camp they fired a number of shots, but they could not follow us in the night. I was hoping that you had heard them."

I shook my head. I had been so deep in thought that I must have missed the shots entirely. Even if I had heard them, I do not know what I would have done.

"Our worst fear," the professor continued, "was that you would be discovered. Abdul darted down the side passage. It must have been used by priests thousands of years ago and has a peephole by which they could have looked into the room."

He brought me over to the wall. Above the stone used as a torch holder a small opening led into the darkness. It was the place the Arabs had marked as hollow. Abdul had stood behind the wall and cried out in his deep voice. The sound had echoed down around the passage and through the walls.

The first Arab had been killed by a stab in the back. He had been standing close enough for Abdul to reach him with the knife. Our camel driver with the torch, however, required a difficult throw. It had taken tremendous accuracy to perform the feat without striking the walls. Had the knife fallen short, Abdul would have been discovered immediately. As it was, he threw the knife and then snuffed out the light before they could guess what happened. I shook my head. What an incredible man.

By the time we made it back to camp, the first rays of light were beginning to edge over the horizon. Abdul had some soup on the fire and sat gazing absently into the coals as if nothing had happened. I could muster only a "thanks." Even then he looked acutely embarrassed. When I asked him about his uncanny accuracy with the knife, his sole comment was in regard to the light.

"If I had thought it was a very good throw," he said humbly, "I would not have put out the light. As it was, I was afraid I had missed."

In the early morning we went back to the tunnel and dragged out the two dead Arabs. We buried them in rock graves beside the temple. Now there were three fresh graves side by side.

Just as we finished the last grave, a yell from high up on the mountains echoed across the cliffs. I leaped for my revolver. The cry came again. Abdul stood up, squinting in the light.

"Muhammad!" Abdul cried. "It's Muhammad One!"

Abdul yelled back to him. Far up along the mountain ridge was a faint figure, no larger than a dot. The yell came again and then it disappeared.

Shortly before noon Muhammad One, torn and tattered, came limping across the desert floor. We rushed to help him. At the campsite he collapsed. After some fresh water and a brief rest he was able to recount his story. He had heard a strange sound and gotten up in the middle of the night. Once past the campfire he had been jumped from behind. The Arabs had thrown a cloth across his mouth and dragged him off. Halfway into the desert he had managed to struggle free and utter one single yell. Then they had struck him over the head and he had blacked out.

Realizing they had lost their surprise, the Arabs had stolen back into the darkness. Muhammad was sure they would use him as a hostage if they were unsuccessful in breaking into the tomb. When he came to, he found himself bound and gagged in a small cave in the mountains. When his captors did not return the following night, he assumed that they had killed us. Finally he had managed to struggle free. He was looking down upon the valley when he saw someone preparing the graves. At first he was afraid it was the Arabs who were burying us.

We were overjoyed to see him. We spent an hour attending to his wounds and cleaning him up. Slowly he began to feel improved. That night when Muhammad was stronger, we left for Luxor. Traveling in the cool periods of the evening and early morning we made the trip in two days.

A week later we returned to the valley with a large party. The news of our discovery spread through Egypt like wildfire.

For the first several weeks armed guards were posted over the tunnel. By the end of July a complete excavation crew had been assembled, and we could direct our full attention to the treasures of the hidden tomb.

Inside the chamber beneath the floor we found a large burial room with a sarcophagus and many, many priceless articles of treasure. There were jewelry chests filled with bracelets, rings, and gold pendants of incalculable value. Strange and delicate statues lined the floor. In one corner was an entire box of lapis lazuli figurines. Once these are fully cataloged they will be housed in the Cairo Museum. Yet the actual itemizing of the treasures could never replace the initial excitement of the find. That look, peering down through the tiny crack in the floor, seeing for the first time the luster which filled the room, will always be an incomparable memory. Walking down into the chamber with twelve officials and two photographers and a half dozen reporters could not compare to the unique moment of the find.

There is little else to report except that it was indeed a rare discovery, one that should help place more of Egyptian history in proper perspective. Certainly no tomb credited to Khufu had ever been found near Luxor, nor had the ruined temple ever been previously described. The translators who examined the tomb stated that the hieroglyphics referred to a burial ordered by Khufu for one of his high priests, not the burial of the pharaoh himself. Still the size and elaborate decoration of the tomb indicated the priest was of no small importance.

The only other note to report is that we found only two bodies. The first body was that of the priest in the burial chamber beneath the floor. The second was the mummy at the end of the passage between Osiris's feet. This body was smaller and there was speculation that it might be a young man or woman, perhaps even a wife or a relative of the priest. The two empty chambers at the end of the hallway might once have housed other burials, but nothing of value was discovered there.

At the end of August the two bodies were loaded upon a caravan and transported over the mountains through a narrow pass to the Nile. Here they were placed upon a felucca and sent downstream to Cairo.

I was in Luxor when they passed. At the lead was the boat with the priest and the treasure. Many small native boats sailed after it. Word had passed through the surrounding countryside that a great tomb had been found and that the dead priest was being transported to Cairo. Great crowds came forward to see the procession. Men fired shotguns into the air. Women threw sand upon their heads and cried in anguish. It was as if one of their present rulers had died rather than a high priest from 2700 B.C. Yet the tradition of the Egyptian people remains. How strongly they mourn their dead and ancient leaders.

The Egyptian government proved completely unpredictable. At the last minute we were permitted to ship the bodies back to the States. I suspect it was partially due to the coaxing of Abdul, and partially as a reward to the professor. To him, of course, the scientific examination of the bodies was just as important as the treasure.

Upon Muhammad One's return to the village there was a great celebration for him. Abdul insisted that it was only due to his personal bravery that we had made the discovery. I had hoped that he would accompany us back to Cairo, but the demands placed upon him by his family proved too much. He finally decided to remain in Luxor, but I think he was sad to see us go.

At the end of the summer I said good-bye to Abdul. My last official assignment for the professor was to fill out the shipping cards for the two mummies so that they could be forwarded to our university in the States. We used the address: State University Museum, San Francisco, California. They would be the sixth and seventh mummies which the professor had studied. Simply, they were abbreviated SUM VI and SUM VII.

II

Resuscitation

11

UPON OUR return to California *Newsweek* and *Time* wanted interviews. Reilly received a number of speaking invitations and references to our discovery appeared in the papers. Some speculated our treasure might rival that of Tutankhamen, but ultimately the two bodies we brought back would prove of far greater importance than buried treasure. There was still much work to be done, and once the initial excitement was over Reilly was eager to continue with his research.

We were well into the month of October before we unpacked the crates. The two caskets had survived the trip well. One afternoon we unwrapped both mummies down to the inner linen. The smaller of the two, the one I had labeled SUM VI, had been partially ripped open by Arabs searching for jewels. A large rent in the linen exposed the anterior surface of the chest. Upon close examination the texture of the skin appeared brown and hairy. Since most mummified bodies had a characteristic blackish color, caused by the bituminous compounds used in embalming, Reilly was intrigued by our find. The following day we X rayed both mummies. And what a surprise we found!

"The hands, feet, and chest wall look like a boy or small woman," Reilly said, studying the X rays. "But the skull, the teeth?" The teeth came to pointed edges, the jaw and nasal bones were pushed forward almost like a dog.

"And look at this," he said. He ran his finger down the pelvis to a string of small bones which extended from the spine. "A tail! By Christ, Bryan, I think SUM VII is a baboon!"

We reviewed the X rays the next morning with the zoology department. Sure enough the mummified body was a hyrdramis baboon that had probably been placed in the burial complex as a decoy, intended to draw attention away from the secret chamber beneath the floor. The bone plates of the legs and hands showed that the baboon was an adult male. The body had been buried in the typical Egyptian fashion, with the arms crossed, palms flat on the chest. Except where the encasing of the mummy had been ripped open the body was in excellent condition. We never unwrapped it further. It is currently on display with its illustrative X rays in the anatomy museum of the medical school.

We now turned our attention to the larger mummy which had been buried in the hidden chamber. The body was X rayed in three sections. By holding the films together we could view the skeleton in its entirety. It was unquestionably that of a human. A small burial necklace was still around the neck. Three bracelets, visible as bright opaque areas on the X ray, were on the right arm, and two were on the left arm. We were surprised there were not more jewels. There were no large breast plates such as were often found on other mummies, nor any rings.

The presence of third molars in the jaw and the general appearance of the long bones indicated that SUM VII had been perhaps forty-five to fifty years old at the time of death. The bulk of linen wrappings had lengthened the body to nearly six feet, yet the skeleton was relatively small, measuring only five feet four inches in height.

The pelvic configuration and narrow pelvic outlet showed that the skeleton was male. A soft tissue density between the legs probably represented a penis. (I mention this because on at least one occasion we reviewed a mummy in Cairo and found the penis and scrotum were missing. It was not known whether this happened during the embalming process or whether the man had suffered the fate of castration sometime during his life.)

Of extreme interest was a spiral fracture to the left thigh. Since there was no evidence of healing, we concluded that the leg had been broken at the time of death. On the left temple was a tiny hairline fracture. In addition there were two broken ribs. How, then, had he died?

Putting everything together we decided that SUM VII had either been killed during a battle or had somehow sustained a fall. The location of all the fracture sites on the left favored the theory of a fall in which he simultaneously had broken his skull, left ribs, and left leg. Either he had died from a hemorrhage in the brain adjacent to the skull fracture, or he had died from internal bleeding from injuries to his abdomen; whatever the case he certainly had not come to a peaceful end.

Reilly was delighted. The X rays revealed a bone structure far better preserved than he had expected. Faint shadows hinted that some of the internal organs were present, though to what degree of preservation we could not tell. With other mummies we had found sand and matted herbs stuffed into the cavities, which sometimes made interpreting the X rays difficult.

After reviewing the X rays Reilly decided we should begin the unwrapping as soon as possible. Three other graduate students assisted with the procedure. We began one night after dinner. An eerie silence prevailed throughout the amphitheater. The body rested upon a narrow dissecting table brightly illuminated by a row of overhead lights. Very carefully Reilly began to cut through the outer wrappings. We had no idea what to expect. Some mummies crumble into dust at the first exposure to air. Others flake to dried crust at the slightest touch.

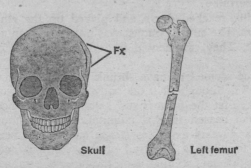

Figure 3. Illustrative X rays, SUM VII. Department of Anatomy. J. Arnold Reilly, M.D. X ray # 75206, 75208

Starting from the bottom the professor slipped a sharp dissecting knife between the legs. At first the yards of wrapping linen separated easily. He worked very slowly, cutting away at the space between the legs until the thighs were freed. Then he moved toward the feet. Carefully lifting the linen he cleared first the ankles, then the heels. In places the preservative gum was so adherent that he had to chip it off. It was more like extricating a foot from a cast than unwrapping wound linen. At the end of an hour both of the feet lay upon the table fully exposed.

The preservation was far beyond our greatest expectations. The nails of the toes were in perfect condition. Fine hairs were still present on the calves, and faint outlines of veins in a subtle latticework were visible beneath the skin. But most remarkable, the toes could be moved. There was a soft pliability about them which was almost like living flesh. I wondered what lay beyond. How would we find the rest of the body: the arms, the chest, the head?

Gently sliding the blade between the wrappings Reilly cut up the midline. First the arms came into view. We uncovered the elbows, as they laid across the chest, before proceeding along the forearms, until we reached the wrists. Then we stopped and removed the rest of the linen from the abdomen. At the navel a small bouquet of tiny purple flowers had been placed. Their fragrance suddenly burst upon us, filling the air with perfume.

Reilly reached down and picked up the clump of flowers. The entire bouquet was no bigger than a man's thumb. They fragmented into powder as he touched them.

Time seemed to have shrunk until it no longer existed. The thought that the body could be so well preserved, that the flowers still held their fragrance, that life had ceased in this mummified shell almost five thousand years ago, was staggering. It had been one thing to stand in the Hall of the Colossus and look out at the stars shining upon the faces of strange gods.

But here, in familiar surroundings, the strange body seemed even more unreal.

Yet Professor Reilly was unmoved. He stopped scarcely long enough to touch the flowers before continuing upward, until the linen lifted away from both wrists, and the bracelets came into view. The deep blues and greens that erupted from the dust-laden bandages dazzled our eyes. I had seen similar bracelets in the museum in Cairo, but never with such brilliant stones. Three of the bracelets were carved in the shape of the eye of Horus. The other two bracelets were composed of rare gems with finely worked figures in gold relief.

Like the feet the hands were in a state of rare preservation: the fingernails intact; the veins and wrinkles standing out across the skin. Most remarkably the fingers could be curled into an "O" and straightened out again. It was fast becoming apparent that we were uncovering a unique specimen.

Yet there was still one area left to be uncovered, and for the first time the professor hesitated. All of us shared his fears. The body was preserved to a degree far beyond our wildest expectations. But what about the head? If the face was poorly preserved, or if it had the appearance of some awful caricature, the entire unwrapping would be a disappointment. Actually the head was of no great importance to our studies; but it was no longer easy to look upon this astonishing body as something dead and inanimate. Would the eyes be open? Would the lips be parted in some last anguished cry? For each of us, the fear of death lay buried within these last yards of wrappings.

The bandages came away from the neck and uncovered the necklace we had seen on the X ray. It was made of a thin gold cord connecting polished blue stones. Professor Reilly did not remove the necklace but continued working the bandage up and across the chin.

When he reached the mouth he cut slowly, until the lips came into view, then the nose, the cheekbones, and finally the eyes. With one single movement he lifted the remaining linen. The face was uncovered.

The chin was strong and well formed. The lips were closed. The nose came down in a broad line spreading out into two fine nostrils. The ears were large and elongated, almost out of proportion to the rest of the head. The hair was short, curled, and gently matted. The eyes were closed, as if the owner of the body had decided to rest and was calmly sleeping.

"It's perfect!" the professor gasped. We stared speechlessly at the body. The early Egyptians had developed a way of embalming which, at least in this one case, had withstood the ravages of time.

12

By midnight we had removed all the linen wrappings, taken a number of photographs, and placed the mummy in a humidity-controlled chamber. At first Reilly wanted to progress with the autopsy in order to study the internal organs, but he decided to postpone it in order to undertake a series of experiments. It was these tests that ultimately revealed just how unique the preservation of SUM VII was.

He began by studying the body through a computerized scanner. The device works somewhat like radar. X rays are used and the various echoes of cross sections of the body are displayed in bright and vivid color on a television screen. The body of SUM VII was placed upon an examining table, then gradually passed through a large donut-shaped scanner, starting at the chest and working down toward the abdomen.

"At least he has a heart," Reilly grunted. Cross sections of the abdomen revealed that the liver, pancreas, and stomach were also intact.

Reilly went back over the colored images carefully. "Very, very strange," he muttered. "I thought for sure that most of the internal organs would have been removed to facilitate preservation. Everything seems present."

He sat lost in intense concentration before sliding back in his chair. "Let's take some deep core samples," he said. "Maybe we can get something to grow."

I knew there were references in the medical literature which indicated that some mammalian cells might be revived after long-term storage. Usually they involved tissues that had been frozen. The chances of getting cells to grow from a dry and desiccated body were extremely slim. Yet Reilly, in his usual meticulous fashion, felt the experiment might prove interesting. A negative finding to him would be just as meaningful as a positive one. "Never assume the obvious," he told me.

That afternoon I took small samples of skin from the Egyptian. Using a very thin knife and gently scraping a piece of tissue from the left leg, I transferred the layer of epithelial cells to a Petri dish with a nutrient gel favorable for growth. Under Reilly's direction I also took some deep tissue samples. On the legs, the thighs, and the lower abdomen I inserted a small probe two to three inches beneath the skin. The device pinched off tiny amounts of tissue which were plated on a nutrient agar and exposed to a wide variety of bacteria.

A week later we went over to the tissue culture laboratory to review our results with Professor Markham. He was an elderly man who walked with a limp. During the past decade he had been nominated on two occasions for a Nobel prize. When he spoke there was a slight hoarseness to his voice. "J. Arnold, I've never seen anything like it," he said. "We've plated a number of bacterial strains on the specimens and there is no growth. The bacteria seem inhibited by the cells of the Egyptian."

He held up a dish of pink agar. No matter how wildly or how luxuriantly the bacteria grew across the agar, they always stopped when they reached the tissue specimens. There was a clear zone of inhibition around each sample.

"Must be some type of antibiotic," Reilly remarked. "I wonder if that is why the body is so well preserved."

The decomposition of a body depends upon both the proteolytic enzymes released from dying cells and the action of bacteria. If somehow the Egyptians had hit upon a preservative which acted as a very potent antibiotic, it might prevent the bacteria from digesting and breaking down the dead cells. But no antibiotic was 100 percent effective. Most of those which worked well on some bacteria were completely ineffective with others. And then there were fungi and viruses to contend with. All of these microbial agents contributed to decomposition. No, there must be something else, I thought.

"How about the tissue samples from the deep probes?" I asked.

Markham motioned for us to follow him through the lab. In a back room was a huge electron microscope. Here a dozen tiny knobs were connected to a display screen. The console looked like the cockpit of an airplane. Next to the screen was a thick-barreled vacuum tube in which the specimens were coated with gold electrons. Images of the specimens could be illuminated upon a television screen at a magnification of one hundred thousand times.

Markham placed a specimen in the holding chamber, then illuminated its image upon the screen. Suddenly a sample so small that it was no bigger than a pinpoint was blown up to fill the screen, looking like the landscape of the moon. We followed the contour of the tissue up a long ridge then over a mountainlike peak into a valley. Three red cells passed the screen like huge biconcave disks. At the bottom of the valley Markham suddenly stopped at a strange, white, amoebalike structure. It was oblong with long thin arms extending from its base.

"This is a white cell," Markham said, "part of the body's defenses." He zoomed in closer so that we could see the fine structure of the cell. "The remarkable thing is the perfect preservation, even at the highest magnification. This specimen is from the left arm of your Egyptian. If you had given me a sample from your own arm there would be some disruption of the cells, some breakdown of the fine molecular structure. But here it is perfect. It is almost as if everything is dormant, as if somehow the clockwork of life has suddenly stopped with the spring still wound."

"There is one other thing." Markham stood up slowly and limped out of the room. Inside the main culture lab he moved to an incubator tray and pulled out a long drawer full of Petri dishes. He

opened a dish in which a faint brownish film had begun to grow across the center.

"Because of the perfect preservation we took some
of the cells and plated them on the agar to see if they
would grow . . ."

He paused and looked at Professor Reilly. His voice
lowered to a whisper. "Life is still there!" he said.
"There has been growth in every sample."

It was midnight by the time we walked together
back across the campus. The faint melody of chimes
drifted down from the college tower. Scattered students hurried toward their dorms.

"Bryan, there are a few things I would like to ask
you," Reilly said.

"Sure," I nodded.

"I would appreciate it if you do not mention any
of the experiments you have seen tonight to anyone.
Not to your friends or roommates or anyone else. It
may be some fluke of the laboratory. I would rather
not have the word get around that we have come upon
some unusual findings."

He stared at me, his eyes searching into my face.
"Can I trust you to do that?" he asked. "I'll get in
touch with you again when I feel the timing is right
to continue with our work. For the present let's bring
everything to a halt."

"But, sir," I protested.

He shook his head. "We must proceed very, very
cautiously. We may be on the brink of something . . ."
He paused without continuing his sentence. "I am
sorry," he said finally. "Please understand. There
are a few things I need to think out before we can go
on."

"All right," I answered. I tried to smile but I felt
terribly disappointed. We had barely scratched the
surface. I could not believe Reilly was going to stop
now; yet something seemed to be churning violently in
his mind. Whatever it was, he elected not to tell me.

The next week I buried myself in my studies.
There were grand rounds, attending lectures, and student assignments to be completed. I called the anat-

omy lab on two occasions. During the first call
Reilly was in the middle of a lecture and could not
come to the phone. On the second he had gone East
for a conference. I could find out nothing. Ms. Jacobson would only say that he was well and had no work
for me at the time.

A month passed before I heard from the professor
again. It came in the form of a note from the dean.
They were having a special meeting of the faculty
on Sunday morning and Professor J. Arnold Reilly
had requested that I attend.

13

THE MEETING on Sunday morning was most unusual. First because the dean rarely called someone in to discuss a school matter on the weekend, and second because Dr. Reilly's name was on the invitation. In thinking it over I suspected we both might be due for some severe criticism from the faculty on our work with SUM VII. Medical schools get very edgy about unwarranted publicity, especially in regard to research that involves scientific speculation. Professor Reilly, however, had a solid reputation and was well respected by everyone in the medical community. I was sure they would not reprimand him. But why was I invited unless something had gone wrong?

I arrived early and seated myself in the dean's waiting room. Soon several members of the faculty appeared. The dean's secretary offered us coffee and invited us into the conference room. Over the next ten minutes a dozen other professors arrived. Grayhaired Professor Markham limped in past me. He was followed by Dr. Patterson, chairman of radiology, Dr. Harkness from the pathology lab, Dr. Beeson, the cardiac surgeon. Almost every major department in the university hospital was represented.

For a few moments there was quiet chatter, then Professor Reilly and Dean Chapman walked into the room. Instantly talk ceased. From the expression on Reilly's face all was not well. He looked worried and strained, but he smiled faintly at me before taking a seat.

The dean was a tall, handsome man with blond hair, who had been a college athlete, an all-American, somewhere back East. He was in his middle forties, still very much in the prime of life.

"Gentlemen, I cannot impress upon you enough the

seriousness of this meeting," Chapman began. "All of you in one way or another have been aware of the research which Professor Reilly has been performing on SUM VII. You are also familiar with some of the inexplicable phenomena which he has found. I wanted to bring you here so that you can help guide us from the very beginning. There are many years of clinical experience in this room. We want to tap your judgment, to use your wisdom. At all costs, however, I would like to request your utmost secrecy in the matters we are about to discuss."

I glanced around the table. Professor Beeson pulled slowly at his chin. Dr. Markham nodded silently. Reilly stared solemnly across the table.

"Dr. Reilly?" Chapman nodded.

The anatomist stood up. He paused for a moment, as if carefully picking his words. "We have known from the beginning," he said, "that there were certain differences between SUM VII and every other mummy we have dealt with. If the cell scrapings could survive, we wondered about the possibility of the internal organs. We wondered further what effect certain nutrients might have.

"In the human body the easiest access to all of the cells is through the arterial venous system. These provide large-bore channels throughout the body. The biggest question was their patency. In death these vessels become clogged. One day last week we spent four hours using a physiological solution to flush clots from the vascular tree. Once we finished we injected the arteries with a radio-opaque dye."

He turned on the light in an X ray view box. It flickered for a moment until all the panels lit. Then he pulled out a series of X rays and flipped them onto the screen.

"Let me direct your attention to a few of the details," he said. "On the right side," he pointed, "you can see the flow of dye down the main arteries. On the left there is a fracture and some disruption around the vessels, but they continue intact to the foot. To our surprise we illuminated the inferior vena cava all the way up to the heart. Now look at the capillary filling across the lungs."

A gasp of amazement arose from the table. The lungs had filled in the tiny lacework pattern of the alveoli. The vessels were patent and perfectly preserved.

"Spurred on by the initial pictures we came back and injected the carotid arteries on both sides of the neck."

He showed two additional X rays of the brain. The dye inside the cerebral vessels lighted up like streets on a city map. "On the left side of the brain," Reilly said, "there is a small indentation of the vessels. This man suffered a skull fracture over the left temple. There is evidence here that he sustained a small hemorrhage next to the fracture.

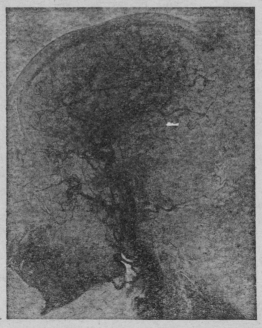

Figure 3a. Arteriogram showing patent cerebral vessels of Sum VII. Contrast injection ® carotid. Dept. of Radiology, University Medical Center.

"To verify this we made a burr hole through the left temple and removed a large amount of clotlike debris. He had indeed bled into the brain. It appears that he died from a cerebral hemorrhage. We suspect that the initiating cause may have been an aneurysm. In either case we think he subsequently fell, causing the fracture to the skull, the ribs, and the left femur."

He stopped to readjust an X ray on the view box.

"In summary the vascular system appears patent. There are no major obstructions or disruptions. The lungs, heart, and brain all seem to fill well . . ."

Reilly paused. "Gentlemen, I would like to introduce the following proposal: If the vascular system is intact; if indeed some of the cells in the body of SUM VII show certain signs of life; then perhaps we should try to restore the circulation . . ."

A murmur rose from the table. Suddenly everyone began speaking at once. The room disrupted into total confusion.

"Gentlemen! Gentlemen, please!" Dean Chapman shouted. "Please give us your attention. This matter is for serious consideration."

"But what would you expect to find?" someone asked.

"I don't know," Professor Reilly shook his head. "If we are lucky . . . very lucky, perhaps a few organs would respond. If not, at least we would have given it a try . . ."

Everyone tried to speak at once. There were a dozen questions. Finally a deep voice boomed out.

"Reilly, this is preposterous!" A heavyset gentleman stood up. He was Dr. Roger McDermitt, the chairman of orthopedics.

"You men aren't dealing with any average patient. You talk about him as if he walked into your office five minutes ago. This man has been dead for five thousand years! This whole thing verges on the most exaggerated form of quackery."

Again the room erupted. There were more questions, more arguments. Voices were raised. Chapman rapped his hand against the table. "Quiet!" he shouted.

"I appreciate all of your comments. That is the reason we called you here. But I think we need to proceed in an orderly fashion. I would like to hear from each of you, one at a time, starting with Dr. Beeson."

The cardiac surgeon rose quietly. He began easily, as if discussing a case on rounds. "Well, you know with open-heart surgery we replace the circulation all the time. It would be technically feasible to hook up a heart-lung machine to the body and supply oxygenated blood."

"Do I understand you would condone such an experiment?" McDermitt cried, a shocked tone to his voice.

The cardiac surgeon frowned. "I think we are at a point in medicine where we should advance. It is as simple as that. If we find the right preparation I don't think we should wait any longer. Yes, to answer you simply. Yes, I think it would be worth a try."

"But the heart itself, how would it beat?"

Beeson shrugged. "We would have to restore the circulation first. Then we could see. Perhaps we would have to use a pacemaker, perhaps a transplant."

"That is ridiculous!" McDermitt scoffed. "Can you imagine convincing some parents to sign a donor permit to transplant the heart of their nineteen-year-old daughter into a five-thousand-year-old mummy?"

Everyone laughed. McDermitt had not intended to make his comment funny, but it was a needed relief from the intensity of the discussion. Dean Chapman interrupted again.

"Of course there are many physiological implications of such a move. I think this morning we should hammer out some criteria if we are to proceed with the project. First of all, should we go ahead with the experiment? If so, how much money should we spend? What lengths should we go to to restore life if that seems a possibility? Has there been, was there, so much brain damage that there might be no mental return even if we could restore the circulation? These are all questions we should discuss and decide."

"I know what all of you are thinking," Dr. Reilly added. "We certainly do not want a mindless vegetable hooked up to a mechanical device with no hope for recovery. But even then you are assuming a great step. That we could restore any type of life is a significant breakthrough."

There were several nervous coughs.

"What about introducing new bacteria into the operating room? Exposing patients to virulent strains that might have changed over the ages. Ones that perhaps are much more dangerous to us than they were to the Egyptians?"

Reilly nodded. "There is always that risk," he said, "but let me remind you that all of the cultures we have taken have not grown anything at all. Not even from the inside of the wrappings. Something about the tissues of SUM VII seems to inhibit bacterial growth something we have not yet identified. Right now I think we are safe. Certainly we would have to use sterile precautions to prevent contamination in either direction, both for the patient and ourselves."

"And what do you plan to do if you get the heart restored and the body alive? Then what?" McDermitt protested.

"Put him in the intensive care unit," Beeson answered. "Treat him like any other patient with open-heart surgery."

"Gentlemen, I would like to say a word of caution," a new voice spoke out. We all turned to see Dr. Wallace, the chairman of psychiatry stand up. "I have not said much until now because those matters which have been discussed have dealt mostly with technical procedures. I would like to caution you, to remind you that the Egyptian was once a man. He had the same desires, the same thoughts, the same feelings as you or I. Imagine what would happen if you are totally successful—you will be transporting him abruptly from an age five thousand years ago. Our present society may have little to offer him. I am not sure a man, any man, can make such a trip and remain sane. I must caution you that he is not a dog, or a cat, or some experimental animal which has been raised in the lab, but a member of our own species. His life and his death should be respected as such."

The psychiatrist had spoken in quite a simple fashion. Perhaps he was right. The shock might be too great. But how could you tell? A long silence followed his words. Slowly the discussion resumed. For three more hours it raged back and forth and when all the topics were exhausted, Dean Chapman called for a vote. The proposal carried, eleven to four.

In the end it was Dr. Beeson, the cardiac surgeon, who spoke most strongly for proceeding.

"Look," he said, "I'm willing to give it a try. Think what people would have said fifty years ago if we had proposed the transplantation of the human heart. They would have laughed us out of the building. And now we have completed more than a hundred such operations. We have the technology. On the short side, if we fail—we have lost nothing. It is my operating room and my team that will do the work. On the long side, if we are successful . . . if somehow there is something there that we can bring back . . . then I think we will have to go back to the textbooks and rewrite the definitions of life. It's my educated guess that nothing will happen. I doubt that we will prove anything at all. But we have an opportunity unequaled in the history of medicine. It is our duty to follow it up. As humans, as scientists, as physicians . . ."

After the meeting I walked with Dr. Reilly back toward the anatomy lab.

"Bryan, I'm sorry we had to do some of this work without you," he said. "I was moving into an awfully speculative area. There might have been some severe criticism, and I did not want you involved."

It was a typical response for him. I should have expected it.

"Anyway it looks like we got past the major hurdle," he said. "Now that we have a green light from the faculty, Beeson wants to schedule the operation for next weekend. We'll only have to hope that no one blows it to the press."

"How do you propose to communicate with him?" I asked.

Reilly laughed. "You sound as if you were already predicting success."

I shrugged. "If you had told me four months ago when we were crawling through those tombs in Egypt that we would ever be involved in this kind of a medical project I would have told you that we had all gone mad."

"Maybe we have," Reilly answered slowly. "Maybe we have."

14

_____

ON WEDNESDAY evening Professor Reilly asked me to come to his house to discuss some interesting news that he had received. We took coffee in the study.

"Have you ever heard of 'Letters to the Dead'?" he asked.

I shook my head.

"A strange custom," Reilly answered. "In a number of burial sites excavators have found certain letters which appear to have been placed there after the death of an individual, asking the deceased for help. Usually they were written by loved ones or intimate friends. Often they were placed in the graves at great risk."

He reached forward on his desk and produced a thin envelope. The stamp was from Egypt. The letter had been written on official government stationery with an Arabic inscription on the side.

"Yesterday I received this letter from Abdul," Reilly said.

He handed it over so that I could read.

Most honorable professor:

I am thinking you will find this of great interest. This past week workers going through the tomb in the Valley of the Sphinx found a small alabaster jar. It was half-covered by rocks and partially buried at the entrance to the underground chamber.

Inside was a very old parchment which appears to be a "Letter to the Dead." I have asked Samir Muhammad, curator of the Egyptian Museum, to translate the message. He thinks the letter was brought into the tomb five or six months after the underground chamber was sealed.

Unfortunately some of the letter is lost. The paper is coming apart like ash. He could translate only with the greatest difficulty. I have rewritten that which is legible for your eye.

MY BELOVED. I HAVE MISSED YOU SUCH THAT WORDS CANNOT DESCRIBE THE EMPTINESS WHICH FILLS MY HEART . . . [words smeared and unintelligible] . . . THE PRIESTS ARE EXTREMELY JEALOUS AND DO MUCH IN THEIR POWER TO SWAY MY FATHER'S MIND . . . [message smeared] . . . THE GREAT HOUSE IS NEAR COMPLETION BUT THE WORK GOES SLOWLY SINCE YOUR FALL. ALREADY THE WORKERS HAVE BUILT A SMALL SHRINE AND NOW MY FATHER HAS BEGUN TO TALK OF BUILDING A GREAT MONUMENT FOR YOU WHICH WILL FACE THE RISING SUN. A MONUMENT IN THE SHAPE OF A LION . . . [figures obscured] . . . PRAY FOR MY CHILD. THE SEED IS GROWING STEADILY IN MY BODY . . . I HAVE GREAT FEAR NOW THAT YOU ARE GONE. I PRAY THAT YOU WILL COME BACK.

[SIGNED WITH THE ROYAL CARTOUCHE]
MANARKOS

"Manarkos was the daughter of Khufu!" Reilly said. "She must have been carrying SUM VII's child. Some of the facts about our strange priest are beginning to come to light."

As I read the message I wondered what had happened. It seemed that our assumption about the death of SUM VII was partially correct. He had died from a fall. Had he been working on some structure when the aneurysm in his brain had ruptured and had he tumbled off? From the extent of the injuries on the X rays he had obviously fallen a great distance. But what did the letter mean about the Great House? Had he fallen from the Great Pyramid during its construction?

The Pharaoh Khufu had a number of wives and a

large number of children. Upon his death there was tremendous unrest in the country, and the line of succession changed several times. Had the priest we found been part of some inner-palace intrigue? And what had happened to the child?

I turned back to Abdul's letter.

The curator has further sent two men to the valley to translate the hieroglyphic pictures on the walls of the corridor. He agrees from all of the findings that the burial beneath the chamber is a high priest. According to the curator the pictures depict a man found wandering half-dead in the Nubian wastes. After he was restored to health, it became apparent that he was capable of great feats of magic. The hieroglyphics state that he could "calm wild beasts" and "turn a man to stone." When the Great Pharaoh (Khufu) heard of this he called the man forth to be examined by his priests. They were so amazed they made him a member of the court, first as a consultant and later as a priest. At the end he was full adviser to the pharaoh on all matters concerning architecture, astronomy, and mathematics.

One of the hieroglyphics shows the priest represented as a lion with a man's head. The curator poses the interesting speculation that this might be a symbol used to represent the Sphinx.

I am hoping that you will find this of interest. I remain

Your most humble servant,

Abdul

"Well?" Reilly said.

I sucked in my breath. "Incredible," I answered. "It certainly adds a new dimension to our find."

Reilly nodded. "It is very, very tempting to associate the priest with the Sphinx. As you know, the monument is thought to have been built sometime after the Great Pyramid. Scholars have been debating its origins for centuries."

"The rocks which Muhammad One used to find the burial site looked like the figure of a sphinx as well," I suggested. "A lot of it seems to fit."

"It makes interesting speculation, but probably we will never know. The pictorial drawings on the walls of tombs were often exaggerations meant to carry some idea of the life of the deceased into eternal judgement. This business about the priest being 'found in the sand' and the statement about his being 'full adviser' to the Pharaoh Khufu may be grossly exaggerated. The 'Letter to the Dead,' however, is not so easily dismissed. It is a very important find."

I looked at the photographs of the pyramids on the professor's wall. For five thousand years they had guarded their secrets closely. Now we were on the verge of bringing back the past, not by spade and shovel but by the technical advances of modern medicine. In less than ninety-seven hours we were going to hook the great high priest of the Pharaoh Khufu to a cardiac bypass machine. The ancient Egyptians had believed that life was everlasting, that one day the soul would return to the body. Were we finally making it all come true?

15

As THE weekend approached, I thought constantly of the strange body we had uncovered; and when Sunday morning arrived, I nervously said good-bye to my roommates, pretending that I was going to the library. I walked to the main hospital, where I spent a half hour pacing in the student recreation center before I took a deep breath and climbed the two flights of stairs leading to the surgical dressing lounge. Two orthopedic residents had just finished a case and were taking off their gowns. I smiled meekly at them and proceeded to the observation tower.

A large audience was already present. The dean of the medical school and Professor Reilly were there, along with the other faculty members from our meeting the week before. Below the glass panels SUM VII lay on the operating table, white and cold. One of the nurses scrubbed a red betadiene solution across the groin. A second nurse spread the antiseptic solution across the chest, where it flowed down the sides of the body like red syrup. Here they would connect the cardiac bypass tubes. The nurses repeated the scrub three times, going back over the same areas in widening circles.

An anesthesiologist and his assistant were at the head of the table. Dr. Becson paced with his arms folded, gazing absently across the room. Three other assistants stood in the corner whispering.

A large monitoring device was next to the wall. Three flat lines rode across the screen with monotonous repetition. These would measure the pulse, the blood pressure, and the electrical activity of the heart.

A second monitoring device, an EEG, used to

measure the electrical activity of the brain, was being connected to the scalp by a neurologist. A dozen small leads were inserted into shaved portions of the head corresponding to twelve parallel lines which moved across the graph of the machine's central recorder. Next to it a third device measured the body's temperature, in centigrade, through an electrical probe inserted in the rectum. The number five flashed upon a screen in bright orange print.

As I sat down, Professor Reilly came over. "This should be a big day, Bryan," he said.

I nodded slowly. The whole idea had become frightening to me. It seemed to touch a core of existence that we humans are not supposed to deal with.

There was a sharp rap on the microphone. Dr. Beeson looked up at us from the operating-room floor.

"Gentlemen, I think we are about ready to proceed."

He turned to his team. They moved quickly, draping green sheets across the body so that only two areas of skin were visible, the chest and the right groin. It might have been the beginnings of a normal open-heart operation at any major hospital, with one exception—all measurements of electrical activity were absent.

Taking a scalpel Beeson made a long vertical incision down the sternum from the upper portion of the chest toward the abdomen. There was no blood; the tissues parted as if he were cutting a loaf of bread. Using a small electric handsaw he proceeded to cut through the bony portion of the sternum.

"Tissues seem compliant," he said. "I keep wanting to ask the anesthesiologist about the blood. It's a hell of a bad sign when we are operating. No blood usually means the patient has expired." He laughed at his own joke. None of the rest of us smiled.

Down at the right groin his assistants had completed the cutdown into the femoral artery and vein and were now dissecting the area clear. In a few moments a long polyethylene tube was brought up and attached to the artery and a second was placed into the vein.

After the chest cavity was open, Beeson thrust a large metal retractor into the incision and steadily spread the device with his fingers until the heart came into view. "Anatomy seems normal," he said. He felt down across the heart. "Right atrium and ventricle intact but small."

More polyethylene tubes were inserted into the outflow chambers of the heart. Two technicians crouching over the blood pump machine worked steadily with the dials, and soon a thin clear liquid flowed into the groin vessels. In a few minutes it began to return through the tubes connected to the heart.

"Our plan is first to infuse the circulation with a highly oxygenated solution," Beeson said.

"It provides oxygen for the tissues, then returns to the pump and washes free excess metabolites. Once this solution flows satisfactorily we will switch to blood. We will start with a low temperature to keep the tissue demands to a minimum and gradually work up. We cooled the body just before the operation. The clear solution which you see running in is kept at near freezing."

Beeson stopped and looked over at one of his technicians. "Temperature now?"

"Ten degrees centigrade," the technician answered.

We watched the monitors. The needles from the EEG rode quietly and steadily across the graph paper. The measurement on the oscilloscope recording cardiac activity was also a straight line. Five minutes passed. No one moved.

"Pump resistance," Beeson barked.

"Down, sir," one of the technicians answered. The infusion fluid had gradually permeated through all of the vessels and was now returning to the outflow tracks.

"All right," Beeson said, "let's go on to oxygenated blood."

On Beeson's command a pump technician opened a valve and a line of liquid red spurted up through the transparent tubes leading into the femoral vein in the right groin. Three minutes passed before one of the tubes exiting from the heart began to turn pink.

Slowly the infused blood was making its way through the circulation and now returning. The color of the outflow tube gradually changed from a faint pink to a rose then to a bright red.

"Circulation intact," Beeson said. His voice was matter of fact. His commands were given without emotion.

"Raise the temperature," he ordered, stepping back and folding his hands. "Not much for us to do now but wait."

"Temperature now twenty," the technician announced.

The numbers of the temperature on the digital display changed slowly, moving like minutes on a computer clock.

21 . . . 22 . . . 23 . . . 24 . . .

"We'll begin to slow down the increments of warming now," Beeson said "As we approach thirty degrees the temperature changes will become critical. This is when the first responses should occur."

A half hour passed as the numbers on the temperature console crept gradually upward from twenty-six to twenty-eight and then to thirty. But nothing happened. The lines all rode across their display screens without the slightest change.

Reilly was sitting on the edge of his seat staring into the operating room. A heavy frown had pushed its way across his face. Dean Chapman was biting the corner of his lip. Dr. Markham had been smoking a pipe but now he too had stopped, as the smoke twisted slowly from the bowl toward the ceiling. Only the orthopedic surgeon, Professor McDermitt, seemed pleased. It was as he had predicted. The entire experiment was a colossal waste of time. Nothing would happen at all.

Thick beads of perspiration began to form on Beeson's brow. A nurse came and wiped his forehead with a cloth.

"One more degree," he said quietly.

The temperature on the display screen slowly dissolved from thirty to thirty-one . . .

Ten minutes passed. But what could we really

expect? The body had been dead for nearly five thousand years. Maybe McDermitt was right. Maybe we had all gone mad.

"One more degree," Beeson said. He hovered over the operating table. The temperature changed to thirty-two. The anesthesiologist at the end of the table shook his head. Nothing. Straight flat lines across all the display screens. Beeson looked up toward the audience in the observation tower. There was anger and disappointment in his eyes. He shrugged as if to say that he had tried, that there was nothing more he could do, and then he turned back to the operating table. Just as he did this there was a sudden cry:

"ACTIVITY! Activity on the scope!"

It was true! The line measuring the electrical activity of the heart showed a slight irregularity, as if it had been drawn by a very weak and shaky hand. Then it became flat again.

There were no regular complexes, no well-defined cardiac beats, just this lightest quiver of electrical activity. It had lasted hardly more than a second and then it was gone.

"Thirty-three degrees now," the technician said.

Slowly, as if bobbing upward from a very deep ocean plunge, the small bright dot on the oscilloscope began to fluctuate ever so slightly. Soon the oscillations above and below the base line became broader, the irritability more pronounced. A minute passed. Our institution had performed over a hundred heart transplants, but never, anywhere, had an operation such as this been attempted.

Almost imperceptibly a small blip occurred on the screen, followed by a second. They were very far apart at first. Then a run of three blips. Then nothing. Then a single blip again. Good God, I thought. Was the heart beginning to beat?

The faint repetitive blips on the oscilloscope reminded me of a movie I had seen in medical school which showed the first heartbeats of a chicken embryo. Someone had dissected away part of the shell while the embryo was still inside and the camera showed the rhythm of the embryonic heart. A few beats at first, then with more regularity, until the small transparent tissues were a synchronized beating mass. The beginnings of the rhythm of life, I thought, like the Nile. Rising and flooding, surging forth with its rich life-giving waters, carrying nutrients to the crops and the trees and the living things along its banks. The endless crashing of the waves upon the seas seemed to have this same inherent rhythm. Had we captured that in our lives? In our hearts? Was this a common denominator of life, passed down to us through a hundred million years of evolution?

Suddenly the electrical activity of the heart leaped across the scope in a wild, bizarre electrical pattern.

"Fibrillation!" Beeson exclaimed.

He took a pair of electrical paddles connected to a defibrillation machine and placed them across the heart. Using a low electric current he discharged the paddles. There was no jerk of the body, only the complete cessation of the electrical activity on the monitor. A flat line moved slowly across the screen.

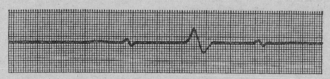

Figure 4. The electrocardiogram of SUM VII showing the first evidence of electrical activity in the heart. (Temperature = 33°C, surgical amphitheater, 2:55 P.M. Attending: Patrick Beeson, M.D., Dept. of Cardiovascular Surgery.)

Had we lost him? Reilly was leaning forward so that his head almost touched the glass window. His eyes were fixed upon the monitoring devices.

"Raise the temperature one degree," Beeson barked. The image on the digital display changed to thirty-four. Inside the open chest of SUM VII the heart contracted like a fist, clenching, pausing, clenching again. A mature complex appeared on the cardiac monitor, repeated itself. Then a run of bizarre beats. Then another complex. With each well-formed beat the graph measuring the pulse pressure began to swing, slightly at first and then with a steady, predictable force.

Suddenly there was a violent swing of the needles measuring the EEG, as if a mass of brain waves had fired off spontaneously. The needle was thrown completely off the graph, thumping against the side of the machine before slowly beginning to drift down toward the midline.

Beeson glanced up at the gallery. "Reilly, I think we may have a live being here." His voice sounded high and unnatural, as if a thread of saliva were stuck somewhere in the back of his throat.

Spontaneously all the observers broke out in a loud, uninhibited cheer. Everyone was on his feet, slapping each other's backs and shaking hands. Reilly was beside himself.

"We did it!" he shouted with tears in his eyes. "By Christ, we did it!"

I wanted to jump, to dance, to shout. It did not seem possible. For fifty centuries the body of SUM VII had lain silently in its tomb. And now the heart of the great high priest beat once again.

16

DURING THE next five days a struggle went on in Room 307 of the Intensive Care Unit that could have been the struggle in special care units in any major hospital on any day. Nurses hovered over the Egyptian; residents were in constant attention; and Dr. Beeson himself spent most of his time closely supervising them all. It was typical that he should encourage Reilly and the rest of us to go out for a triumphant drink following the operation, and then not join us. "Too much work to be done," he said later. For the precarious balance between life and death which teetered within the body of SUM VII had by no means ended with the cardiac bypass procedure. "Even if he leaves the operating room," Beeson had said, "we stand less than a 10 percent chance of success."

Only hospital personnel concerned with his immediate care was allowed into his room, so I had to satisfy my own interest concerning his progress by reading the hospital chart. Finally curiosity overcame me—on the second postoperative day I dressed in hospital greens and tried to pass for one of the cardiac residents. I entered the Intensive Care Unit at ten o'clock at night, when everything was very quiet. The nurses had just finished making rounds.

I grabbed a stethoscope at the central desk and walked boldly into the room. A nurse was adjusting his intravenous line. She wore a mask and was dressed in a sterile gown. A name tag identified her as "Jennifer Hughes, R.N."

"I'm sorry," she said. "He's not allowed any visitors."

"I know," I answered. "I just wanted to see how he was doing."

A glance could tell. He was hooked to a dozen machines. His breathing was controlled by a bellows device which regulated the flow of air. There were several intravenous lines in each arm. A catheter drained his bladder. Two large tubes sucked the drainage from his chest. He did not look well at all.

The nurse walked around the bedside toward me. "You one of the residents?" she asked.

"I helped with his operation," I bluffed.

A pair of blue eyes squinted toward me. Then Jennifer turned back and began working with one of the monitors. She was a beautiful girl. Blond hair peeked out from beneath her cap and her legs were long and slender. She filled out the gown in all of the right places.

"Has there been any progress?" I asked.

She shook her head. "Still comatose. His heart is beating, but that is all I can say."

She did not take her eyes off the monitor. "If you're one of the residents, how come I've never seen you before?"

I tried to think rapidly. "It's because I've been . . . at another hospital . . . on another rotation . . . you see . . ."

She interrupted what she was doing and stared directly at me. "You know Beeson would kill you if he caught you in here?"

"I . . . yes . . . but . . ."

"You're a medical student, aren't you?"

I nodded with a shrug. "I followed him all the way from Egypt. I just wanted to stop in, to see how he was doing. How did you know?"

"Because you're too young for a resident. And because they're always busy and tired and they don't come into a room and gaze around at the ceiling and get their feet caught in the monitoring wires."

I looked down at my feet and tried to shake my left shoe from a loop that had somehow wrapped its way around my toes. I turned beet red.

"I think you'd better go," she said.

I backed out toward the doorway. "I'm sorry. I didn't mean to interrupt you, but I am extremely concerned about his progress."

"I know," she answered. "We all are." And she turned back to her work.

The next day I visited the Intensive Care Unit again, but the door to Room 307 was closed. Through a small glass window I saw Jennifer, though she was too busy to offer much more than a brief smile. From the look on her face things were not going well. The notes at the end of the day showed little improvement. For every inch of progress there had been an equivalent setback.

Tuesday:

9:00 P.M. Two seizures occurred this evening, both treated with Valium. Chest X ray shows no significant improvement. Neurologists feel there has been no change in mental status. Still comatose. Has frequent cardiac irregularity. Beeson considering discontinuation of life-support systems if no further improvement. Prognosis very poor.

> Rooney, M.D.
> Senior Cardiac Resident

On Wednesday SUM VII began bleeding from every orifice. Blood oozed out of his mouth, around the tubes in his nose, through his rectum, and in his urine. He was given twelve units of fresh blood. Twenty-four hours later the bleeding stopped. The body was still alive.

Paradoxically each day that he survived lessened his chances for ultimate recovery. Even though the residents pulled him through these daily crises it became more and more obvious that his problems were ones associated with dying and deteriorating patients. The EEG showed no change from the initial EEG at the time of extracorporeal circulation. He was still comatose. The residents and the nursing staff were becoming fatigued. The picture began to look hopeless. And then a remarkable thing happened, one of those inexplicable events that sometimes occur in clinical medicine.

Friday:

8:00 A.M. PATIENT MOVED! Nurse noted during the night that the patient moved his right hand. EEG this morning shows a pattern similar to delta rhythm (sleep pattern). Heart seems to be stronger. X rays beginning to show improvement of the lungs. One additional seizure treated with Valium.

Lubbock, M.D.
Junior Resident

Saturday:

12 Noon. Patient pulled out endotracheal tube. Seems now capable of breathing on his own. Restless activity has begun, shifting body and legs in bed. At times seems to be waking up! Level of consciousness steadily improving.

Lubbock, M.D.
Junior Resident

Sunday:

8:00 A.M. PATIENT AWAKE! Eyes open and following movement around the room. EEG shows normal alpha waves. Cardiac status stable, X rays continue to improve.

Rooney, M.D.
Senior Cardiac Resident

The following day Reilly asked Beeson if it was all right for us to visit SUM VII in his room. The priest was fully conscious and, although he was very weak, he had begun taking liquid meals. Many of the tubes had been discontinued and he was improving rapidly.

The nurses had shaved his face. He looked distinguished, almost handsome. His eyes opened at the sound of our approach. They were dull blue and strikingly transparent, almost as if there were small mirrors behind the pupils.

He watched us move across the room. Professor Reilly held out his hand and gently pressed the priest's shoulder. "Just wanted to stop by and say hello," he said.

We tried to appear friendly and reassuring.

"Well, what do you think, Bryan?" Reilly asked as we left. There was a broad smile across his face.

I was too moved to be articulate. "He looks almost like any other patient in the hospital," I mumbled.

"Almost the same," Reilly added. "But I don't think I have ever seen a face quite like his. Very peculiar characteristics, especially the eyes. He must be from a most unusual genetic background. It's certainly not a typical Egyptian face."

As we walked down the hall, Dr. Beeson appeared around the corner, accompanied by a half dozen residents.

"Glad to see you," he said. "Got something I think you should see, J. Arnold."

We followed him to a conference room where a series of X rays were illuminated on a view box. There were two different sets of pictures. The first was an X ray of a broken femur separated at midshaft. The fragments were sharply angulated with a sizable distance between the two ends. The second X ray showed another picture of the femur, only this time the fracture line was gone.

"You recognize the films?" Beeson asked.

Reilly stared at them for a moment. "Looks like the left leg of the Egyptian which we took in the funeral wrappings. The second X ray, if it is the same leg, shows marked evidence of healing."

"Healed!" Beeson exclaimed.

Reilly moved closer to see the X ray better. "But how can that be?"

Beeson was smiling. "I showed these films to Dr. McDermitt, the orthopedic surgeon. He thought I was pulling his leg. He accused me of switching films. He had to watch them take another set before he was fully convinced."

Reilly frowned. "How did he explain the changes?"

"He can't." Beeson laughed. "All he could mutter

was 'Incredible! Incredible!' Whatever the case our Egyptian friend there has healed his fracture almost completely in a week. An event unprecedented in medical history, I would say."

"What about the skull fracture?" Reilly asked.

Beeson reached into a pile of films and flipped one up on the board. On the first film the skull fracture was clearly visible over the left temple. On the second film the fracture lines were gone. Complete healing had taken place.

"We're supposed to meet McDermitt at the bedside at one o'clock," Beeson said. "Come on with us. We were just making rounds."

We arrived at SUM VII's room at the same time as Dr. McDermitt. His face was red and he was out of breath. A faint scowl lined his forehead.

"You cardiac guys, always performing miracles," he grunted. He pushed his huge frame in front of us and entered the room. We followed him inside. For the next fifteen minutes he knelt by the bedside of SUM VII and examined his legs. The pulse and color of both extremities were exactly the same. The range of motion was identical. There was no evidence of pain. SUM VII tolerated the manipulation like a passive animal.

"I believe we could try to walk him," McDermitt said. "It looks like he is going to make it despite us."

I was surprised to see the change in the orthopedic surgeon's attitude. In the conference room he had attacked the whole concept of resuscitation. Now he seemed more amazed than anything else.

As they spoke SUM VII watched them, his eyes studying each speaker. I was sure that he had little understanding of what was said, yet he was alert and he seemed amused by the tremendous amount of attention he was receiving. So far he had not uttered a single sound nor made any attempt to speak. He merely watched, patiently and quietly.

Dr. McDermitt stood up from the bedside.

"I've got a conference at two," he said. He looked at his watch, then shook it. "Damn thing must have stopped. What time do you have?"

I checked my own watch. For some reason it had stopped, too. Dr. Reilly took a pocket watch from his vest pocket. "I've got one thirty-five," he said. "But that can't be right."

"You boys should keep up with the times," Dr. Beeson chuckled. We followed him out of the room. He wore a crystal quartz watch with a digital display. "Doesn't lose a second in one hundred twenty-five years," he said. He pushed the button on the display counter. The numbers flashed 1:35. Then he pressed the button which registered the passing of seconds. The number flashed on fifteen and did not advance.

"Damn," he said, a frown of annoyance growing on his face. He knocked the watch lightly on the back of his wrist before glancing sheepishly around. When he pressed the display button again it still registered 1:35.

I looked back into the room. SUM VII had been watching through the doorway with a trace of a smile on his lips.

It took six hours before our watches began to work again.

17

By the end of the second week the Egyptian was doing so well that Beeson decided to transfer him out of the Intensive Care Unit to a special room in the convalescent wing. Here he could be given maximum security, still be monitored, and yet have some freedom to move about. The room was much larger than the one in Intensive Care. There was a small dining area and a nice view of the mountains, and the staff brought in a number of plants and flowers, all intended to make his surroundings as pleasant as possible.

In order to maintain continuity Beeson assigned the same nurses to the Egyptian that had followed him in Intensive Care. A security guard was posted at the entrance of the unit and only certain visitors were permitted into his end of the corridor. So far we had been lucky that no news had leaked to the press, and Beeson was determined that the university remain silent about the matter until the priest had fully recovered. Publicity would bring newsmen, television reporters, and hundreds of other spectators, including a variety of crackpots and gawkers, all of whom might interfere with his progress. Had any rumors begun, the hospital was fully prepared to identify the Egyptian as a foreigner who had come to the medical center for cardiac care. Hundreds of such people arrived from all over the world for open-heart operations every year, and we all hoped that SUM VII would remain hidden anonymously among them.

During SUM VII's first week in the convalescent unit Reilly arranged for me to be given a pass to visit the Egyptian once a day. Since his time was filled with a number of regimented activities—morning lab work, daily chest X ray, daily EKG, daily physical therapy, afternoon sessions with a language specialist, etc.—it was felt that someone who had nothing to specifically test him with might offer some psychological comfort. We were all afraid that the constant tests and intensive therapy might provoke anxiety as he continued to improve.

At first I was afraid to do much more than sit with him or try to show him pictures in a magazine. After a couple of days he recognized me and smiled when I arrived. One day I brought in a small television set and showed him how to work the dials. He was quite intrigued, and it was only then that the frustrations of being unable to talk with him became truly overwhelming. There was a vast difference between our worlds. The thousands of questions going on in both our minds needed answers that were impossible to communicate in any language. So we had to be patient, and wait, and hope that with time we would be able to get through to each other.

As he gained strength he walked with the nurses, strolling up and down the corridors. His demands seemed few, and the hospital staff who attended him all grew to like him. He ate the meals without complaint and, except for meat, which he refused to eat on any occasion, he seemed to tolerate most of the hospital food. Only much later did we learn why he required a strictly vegetarian diet.

His usual evening attendant was Jennifer. One afternoon I met her in the hospital cafeteria. Over coffee she told me of an odd thing the Egyptian had done. She had watched him examine a vase of roses shortly before he retired. Picking them up he had held lightly on to the stems. As he passed his hand over the flowers, each in turn closed its petals and drooped, as if going to sleep.

"He spends hours studying the plants," she said. "It's almost as if he has some type of communication with them."

When I told her about the phenomenon of the watches, she nodded.

"Other nurses have noticed similar things. I think we've all been a little afraid to talk about them. One of the girls swears she was trying to reach out for a vase one morning when it moved in front of her eyes. She reached for it again and it moved again. She finally lurched forward and grabbed it. When she turned around the Egyptian was standing behind her smiling.

"Another nurse told me she was working the morning shift and had stepped out of the room when she heard a sudden explosion. When she rushed back she found him sitting in bed staring at some glassware on a table on the opposite side of the room. His concentration was so intense that he hadn't noticed her. As he continued staring at the table, a second glass exploded, and then a third. The nurse expressed her fright by giving him a severe scolding. As she cleaned up the broken glasses, the Egyptian seemed quite pleased, as if he had successfully completed some kind of a mental exercise.

"It's all a little weird. At times he seems like a normal person and responds like any other patient, at other times he has tremendous mental powers. Sometimes when he looks at me I have the strange feeling that he can read my thoughts. It's as if he can operate at a much higher level than the rest of us."

She paused, staring down into her coffee. "I keep thinking we are going to hurt him," she said sadly, "or that in some way he is going to hurt one of us, and all because of some mistake that we could not predict or identify because we can't communicate with him. It would all be so easy if he could just understand."

Actually SUM VII's progress in English had been rapid. If he was shown a picture of a bird or a tree and told the name, he never forgot it. Yet how could we teach him the meaning of verbs such as "want" or "feel" or "think"? Even with his extraordinary intelligence it would take months of intensive work before we could carry on a reasonable conversation.

As he continued to recover, the need for us to understand his thoughts became increasingly important. At the end of the second week Reilly came up with the intriguing idea of using the computer language lab. For months the linguistic department of the university had been working on a program called BABEL, which attempted to provide a computer translation between languages. Recently they had made news with some translations of an ancient Greek dialect called Linear B. The following Monday I went over to ask for their assistance.

The laboratory occupies an imposing seven-room complex on the top of the new general science wing. Inside are long rows of computer banks. Above the reception desk is a translation from a stone block of cuneiform.

A short, heavyset graduate student with curly hair came out to speak to me. He wore an old corduroy jacket marked with a number of stains, and he introduced himself as Vincent Spanzerelli. His hair sprang from his head in a wild, electric fashion. He had a strange way of listening to me as I talked, cocking his head and letting his eyes wander. Each time I asked a question, they returned to focus on me before he answered.

Realizing I would have to confide in him, I told the story of SUM VII. When I had finished he took me back into the laboratory and sat down.

"Wow," he said. "I'm not sure we can help you." He thought for a long moment, pulling at his chin.

"Do you have tapes of any of his speech?"

"No," I said.

"If we can, we will need to tape a good portion of his conversation. The computer is only as good as we can program. We would need to study the words. Listen to the speech."

He now explained how BABEL worked. The strategy was to convert each language into a common computer code, then translate this in turn into the language desired. In this fashion each language had a common numerical base. Instructions for the placement of verbs, nouns, subjects, and adjectives were specific for each different translation.

We walked over to one of the long computer banks. "You ever see how one of these works?" Spanzerelli asked.

I shook my head.

"We can go from writing into speech and back to writing again," he said. "How's your English?"

"Okay, I guess," I said.

He sat down at a small desk. Working quickly he punched a list of instructions into the computer.

> BABEL PROGRAM. ANGLO SAXON
> LORDS PRAYER SCRIPT 455-8K.
> DISPLAY.

Almost instantly the computer rattled out a typewritten message.

> FAEDER, Ù RE, PÙ PE EART ON
> HEOFONUM, SI PIN NAMA
> GEHALGOD . . .

"Recognize the phrase?" he asked.

I shook my head. It could have been Greek for all I knew. He turned and typed back into the computer.

> BABEL PROGRAM. TRANSLATE:
> PASSAGE SCRIPT 455-8K. ENGLISH,
> WRITTEN MODE.

The machine responded.

> OUR FATHER, WHO ART IN
> HEAVEN, HALLOWED BE THY
> NAME . . .

I shook my head in amazement.

"It's Anglo Saxon English," he said. "Comes from the eighth century A.D. It has more German influence than anything else. This is why we have retained such strong German roots in our present speech. Now listen to this."

He programmed another selection into the computer.

This time, to my astonishment, a strong machinelike voice came over a loudspeaker, in a strange language I could not understand. I listened to the first four sentences, then shook my head. It sounded completely foreign.

Spanzerelli smiled; half-laughing he typed into the computer:

> DISPLAY FOURTEENTH-CENTURY
> ENGLISH, WRITTEN MODE.

The computer responded:

> WHAN THAT APRILLE WITH HIS SHOURES SOTE
> THE DROGHTE OF MARCHE HATH PERCED TO THE
> ROTE, AND BATHED EVER VEYNE IN SWICH LICOUR,
> OF WHICH VERTU ENGENDRED IS THE FLOUR.

"Recognize it?" he asked.

Now it was my turn to smile. It was Chaucer. A passage from the *The Canterbury Tales,* something I had memorized in college. I recognized the written work quickly enough; but spoken, with the proper accent, it had been almost unintelligible.

"That was our own language just six hundred years ago," Spanzerelli said. "The Anglo Saxon base had incorporated French and Latin from the Norman invasion."

I nodded slowly. "And how long do you think it will take to translate an Egyptian tongue spoken five thousand years ago?"

Spanzerelli answered by shaking his head. "There is absolutely no way to tell. Four to six weeks if we are lucky," he answered. "Longer, if not. Maybe it will be impossible. But we need to get some tapes. You will have to get some samples of his speech."

I returned and told Reilly the discouraging news. Without a comparison language for a data base the task would be practically impossible. We were back where we had started.

Yet it was Jennifer who discovered the most simple way to communicate with SUM VII, and I am astonished that we had not thought of it before.

"I was in his room last night," she said, "when I accidentally broke a thermometer and cut my finger. I had thought he was asleep and went over to the sink and ran cold water on it. It was a deep cut, and the blood kept pouring out. Finally I squeezed my finger and held it over my head. Then I heard a clucking sound. When I looked over I saw the Egyptian motioning for me to come to his bedside. As I stood next to him, he gently held my finger in his hand. I thought at first that he'd try to place a bandage on the cut. Instead he took my finger and put it into his mouth! I was so astonished that I jerked away and scolded him. Afterward I felt bad about it because he seemed hurt. But the strangest thing was when I looked at my finger the bleeding had stopped."

She held up her finger. There was a small scar across the bottom of her left index finger. The wound appeared well sealed and there was no evidence of bleeding.

"How does it feel now?" I asked.

"Fine." She smiled. "I didn't even have to put a Band-Aid on it. It seems to have closed off completely.

"Later when I was working on my nurse's notes he stepped out of bed and came over to watch. Something was bothering him. As I finished he made a clucking sound with his teeth, then took the pen from my fingers. Writing very slowly he printed something on the paper.

"I shook my head, trying to tell him that I could not understand. He printed the same message again."

"Good Lord!" I asked. "What was it?"

She reached into her purse and showed me the writing. It was hieroglyphics.

When I showed the figures to Professor Reilly, he leaped up from his chair. "Of course," he exclaimed. "Why haven't we thought of this before?"

That afternoon he called London. In twenty-four hours Professor Reginald Bristol of the British Museum was on a flight to California. Bristol had written several books on early Egyptian languages, comparing the demotic and Coptic scripts, and Reilly had worked with him in Egypt on several occasions. He was considered an expert in hieroglyphics and had done significant work in translating pieces from the temples in Luxor.

At two-thirty in the afternoon we walked into the hospital and started for the convalescent wing. When we entered SUM VII's room we found him sitting by the bed. He nodded politely to us. Reilly introduced the British professor in English. Then we all drew up chairs and sat down.

"We must be very careful how we proceed," Reilly said quietly. "I want him to understand that we are friends, that we are here to help him, that we want to know if there is anything we can do to make him more comfortable."

Bristol took a large pad of white paper from a portfolio. Very slowly he drew some hieroglyphic symbols. He linked these symbols with wavy lines, circles, and dots. The writing was laborious. Fifteen minutes passed before he finished.

SUM VII took great interest in the proceedings. As Bristol finished, however, the Egyptian shook his head. He could not understand them.

"No response to Middle Kingdom figures," Bristol said.

"Older, much older," Reilly whispered. "Go back to the earliest of the Old Kingdom."

Bristol nodded, tore off the page, and started up again. Laboriously he sketched out a new set of figures.*

I watched SUM VII's face. Suddenly his eyes lit up. He nodded, muttering some kind of a guttural sound. I think he finally recognized something we were trying to do. He took the pen from Bristol and sketched out a long line of symbols.

* In written hieroglyphics there is no spacing or punctuation to break the flow of words. The text may be written either vertically or horizontally or from left to right or right to left. The pictures of the various animal symbols always face the starting point. Because of Bristol's familiarity with written English he began by writing from left to right. SUM VII answered each question in the same fashion, until the very end when he began writing from right to left.

My breathing quickened. Reilly leaned forward on the edge of his seat. We were about to open a treasure far greater than any tabloid or temple or statue. Here was a living entity, a man who had walked and lived five thousand years ago!

"Amazing, absolutely incredible," Bristol murmured. "This man is writing from the very oldest texts."

"What is he saying?" Reilly asked.

Bristol took the line of hieroglyphics and studied them carefully. "He says he is from Memphis, that he is a high priest, and he wants to know where he is."

Reilly looked at me and smiled. We had gotten through to him! A flood of questions rushed through my mind, but Reilly held up his hand with a sign of caution.

"We must go very, very slowly," he said. "Ask him his name."

Bristol wrote down the question in hieroglyphics.

SUM VII took the pen and replied with a single drawing. It was a picture of a lion with a head of a man.

"My God," Reilly whispered. "The wall paintings were right. It is the symbol of the Sphinx. He must be Horus-in-the-Horizon, the high priest of the morning sun."

SUM VII continued writing. Carefully he completed a line of hieroglyphics that ended with a cartouche for Khufu.

"I am not sure what he means here," Bristol tried to translate. "He asks, 'Where is a king or pharaoh?' What should I tell him?"

"Tell him Khufu is . . . tell him Khufu is dead," Reilly answered with a grimace. The realization of what we were doing swept over me, like some dreadful storm obliterating the sun. How could we tell him that Khufu was dead, that his whole kingdom was gone, that he had lived five thousand years ago?

As Bristol printed the hieroglyphic message, SUM VII's eyes flickered across the symbols. A frown creeped across his brow. He grabbed the pen and repeated the question.

"I am not sure he believes us," Bristol said.

Reilly paused. "Christ, what can we say? We've got to tell the truth. Write the same thing. He must understand."

Again SUM VII read the message. An expression of gloom flooded his face. His eyes moistened as he took up the pen.

"When?" he wrote.

"When?" Bristol said out loud.

Reilly frowned. "Tell him . . . tell him five thousand years ago."

Bristol wrote the hieroglyphic message. SUM VII read the words. An audible moan came from his lips.

"He must think he is still living then," Bristol gasped.

"It's as if he went to sleep and suddenly woke up. And now he is trying to piece together what has changed."

If we had realized what was happening we would have stopped. We should have paid closer attention to the terrible anguish on the Egyptian's face. In our enthusiasm to communicate with him we had proceeded too quickly. And now it was too late to turn back.

SUM VII took the pen again and began writing. This time he printed quickly and hurriedly across the paper.

"He wants to know about Karsham and Heraditi. He is using the feminine gender here. They are apparently women . . ."

They were girls' names, women that he must have known. I thought of those beautiful wall paintings in the tombs of the Valley of the Kings. There were priestesses and dancers and musicians of incredible beauty, women with tender gentle lines and soft faces.

"Gone, too," Reilly whispered. Bristol wrote down the words in hieroglyphics.

"And Manarkos . . ." SUM VII wrote.

Bristol sounded out the phonetic pronunciation of the word. Reilly looked over at me. It was Khufu's daughter, the one whose signature was on the "Letter of the Dead." She had left a message to him telling of her fears.

Reilly shook his head, and the Egyptian understood. Suddenly his hand began to tremble. "And Memphis and Thebes and Karnak?" he wrote.

"He wants to know about the ancient cities," Bristol said.

"Gone," Reilly said slowly. "Tell him they are . . . gone."

They were once the greatest cities of all Egypt. Now they were nothing more than faint traces in the sand. We might as well have issued him a death sentence. He shook his head violently, then fell back on the bed. The trembling in his right hand became more pronounced.

To my horror I saw the tiny unsteadiness of his fingers begin to spread. It had started with the finest twitch at the distal tip of his index finger before moving up to include his entire hand. Unremittingly the spasm marched in Jacksonian fashion up his arm, first to the wrist, then to the elbow, and finally the shoulder. The total sequence took less than ten seconds.

As the deathlike intensity of the seizure reached his neck and face, he began jerking violently and uncontrollably in a full epileptic fit. His entire body shook, his teeth grated, his tongue rolled around wildly in his mouth. His urine seeped out onto the bedsheets.

"Get a tranquilizer," Reilly yelled. He leaped up on top of SUM VII and pinned him down. "Put something in his mouth," he cried.

I grabbed a corner of the sheet and wadded it up, thrusting it between his gnashing teeth. Bristol ran from the room and instantly returned with a nurse. Only with the greatest effort were we able to hold him still long enough to inject a heavy tranquilizer. Finally the violent jerking stopped, his body relaxed, and his breathing became long and deep.

That afternoon they transferred him back to the Intensive Care Unit. Six more seizures occurred. The cardiac monitors were hooked up, and he was placed on intravenous feeding.

Professor Reilly was extremely upset. "We pushed

him too far," he said. "I should have realized what was happening. I was so amazed that we were communicating with him that I wanted to keep on. I never should have answered his questions. Think of what he could tell us. Think of the secrets locked in his mind. And now . . ."

He placed his head in his hands. His shoulders slumped in the fear that all might be over, that the seizures might have put SUM VII into a convulsive state from which he would never fully recover.

As time passed the Egyptian required still heavier medication. Dosages were given far above the amount used to control normal seizures. The convulsions were becoming harder and harder to stop. Then at six o'clock that evening a strange tranquility came over him. The seizures eased and he passed into a restless sleep.

For six hours he drifted through periods of tremendous agitation, speaking endlessly in languages we had never heard before. The British professor returned to listen. Some of the speech may have been related to Arabic or early Egyptian, but some was in an odd musical language totally distinct from the others. Professor Reilly immediately recognized the opportunity to tape his speech. For the rest of the evening we recorded these outbursts. On one occasion he spoke English, but on reviewing the tapes we found that he was merely mimicking a newcast he had heard.

Around twelve o'clock that night I decided to visit him once more before retiring. The psychiatrist's words were coming back to haunt me: "Our present society may have little to offer him. I am not sure a man, any man, can make such a trip and remain sane."

I found Dr. Beeson leaving the Intensive Care Unit, his head bowed, his gait slow. It looked as if he were at the end of a very long day.

"Is everything all right?" I asked.

He shook his head dejectedly. "The neurologist saw him a few minutes ago. They're concerned that the bleeding inside his brain may have started again, and the heavy dosages of Dilantin we've been giving for the seizures are showing cardiotoxic effects. His pressure has begun to drop. I am not sure he is going to make it."

My mouth went dry. A sickening pain worked its way into my stomach. "What does this mean?" I asked.

Beeson shook his head. "There are so many puzzling things about this case, I don't know what to think. If there is a leak there, we should go back into his brain and clip the aneurysm. The mortality of a second operation is extremely high. If the seizures continue he may have permanent brain damage. We're caught in a very tight place."

Oh, God, I thought. Had he not gone through enough? What was there left for him to live for? Nothing, it seemed now, but our selfish curiosity. We could find out the secrets of the Great Pyramid and the mysteries of ancient Egypt, but only at the expense of great pain to another human being.

"Well, I'm going to get some sleep," Beeson said. He looked very old and fragile. The entire episode was weighing heavily upon us all, perhaps even more than we had realized.

"We'll be lucky if he makes it through the night," he said. "The next twelve hours will tell."

He turned and walked past me. "Good night," he murmured.

I had moved perhaps ten feet up the corridor when a sudden announcement flashed over the public address system.

CODE BLUE. ROOM 307 INTENSIVE CARE UNIT.

The words stunned me. Room 307 was the Intensive Care room for SUM VII. The call was for cardiac arrest.

Beeson had turned and was running up the hall, pounding past me, his breath coming in heavy spurts. I bolted after him, my legs like rubber.

I had witnessed cardiac arrests before and could imagine what the Egyptian would look like. His lips would be purplish, his eyes rolled back. A nurse would be trying to force breath into him, someone else would be pounding on his chest.

People were running from every direction. A chief nurse was shouting instructions, pointing toward Room 307.

Beeson reached the door two steps ahead of me. He raced into the room and stopped abruptly. Two nurses and an intern stood with bewildered looks upon their faces. The cardiac alarm clattered loudly down the hall. More people rushed in behind us.

The three cardiac leads which had been attached to the Egyptian's chest lay limply upon the bed. A line of intravenous fluid was dripping onto the floor while two spots of blood stained the sheets where his arm had been. But the bed was empty. SUM VII was gone.

III

Termination

18

Of ALL the emergencies that may occur in a hospital the cardiac arrest is the most urgent. Once the heart stops, the minutes during an arrest are critical, the seconds precious. Physiologically the average person can tolerate a period of four minutes before irreversible brain damage begins to occur. The pupils dilate. Respiration ceases. Metabolic poisons begin to accumulate in the blood. There is no margin for error, no room for delay.

With this knowledge we had raced to the cardiac arrest in Room 307. The monitoring unit had been set to trigger an alarm at any five second pause between heartbeats. We had arrived less than a minute after the onset of the alarm. What had happened?

It took only seconds to search the room. The windows were closed and locked. The closet was empty. There was no other place for anyone to hide.

"Cancel the code," Beeson growled. He reached forward and turned off the alarm with a distressed look on his face.

"Who was taking care of this patient?"

"I believe it was Miss Hughes," a nurse answered.

"And where is she?" he demanded.

The crowd standing in the doorway parted as Jennifer pushed her way hurriedly into the room. She glanced first at the empty bed, then at the rest of us. Her mouth dropped open. "I . . . I was in charge, sir," she stammered.

"And where is your patient?"

She spoke as if in a daze. "I left the room for just a moment . . . I couldn't have been gone long . . . and then the alarm rang . . . and . . ."

"And then . . .?"

She raised her hand in a futile shrug. "I don't know. . . . I don't know. . . . He was just here. . . . He was right here. . . ."

"Jesus!" Beeson cried. I had never seen him so upset. His face was red. His teeth were clenched. "Christ, if we lose him like this . . . if we find him collapsed in the corner of some hallway . . ."

I think all our thoughts were the same. It was impossible to believe that SUM VII could have gone very far. He was dressed in hospital pajamas. He could speak little English. Moments before we had thought he was in a comatose condition. It seemed impossible that he could be gone at all.

Beeson stood at the nurse's station barking out commands. Telephone calls were made to all the floors. Guards were posted at every exit. No one could leave the hospital without proper identification.

He finally lay down the phone. "St John, I guess we'd better get hold of Dr. Reilly," he said.

I telephoned Reilly at home. He had been asleep and it took a moment for him to realize what had happened. "My God," he finally exclaimed. He wanted to know a thousand details. I could tell him nothing. He said he would come to the hospital right away.

At one-thirty that night Dr. Reilly and I met Dr. Beeson in a small conference room.

"Still no news?" Reilly asked.

Beeson shook his head. "I can't explain it. We've gone back over the thing a hundred times. A nurse leaves the room for a minute. The cardiac alarm rings. Everyone rushes to the room to begin a resuscitation. I was one of the first people to arrive." He shrugged. "I don't know. I don't understand any of it."

"Any clues?"

Beeson shook his head. "I wish that we had even one. Nothing. He has disappeared into thin air."

"Suppose that he left on his own?" Reilly asked

Beeson shrugged. "Could be," he answered. "But when you're as sick as he was, you simply don't get up and walk out of a room. There has got to be some reasonable explanation."

Reilly smiled faintly. "Maybe so, or maybe we just don't understand how he did it. Perhaps he was waiting for the proper moment. It has become apparent to me that he is vastly different from the rest of us. We saw the watches stop that morning on rounds. We saw him heal a fracture in a week. We saw him come back on bypass with a heart which had not beaten for five thousand years. Anything seems possible."

I shook my head. "I don't understand why he would want to leave at all. He is in perfect safety in the hospital."

Beeson frowned. "Safety to you perhaps, but possibly not to him. God knows what it must be like to wake up hundreds of centuries after you thought you had died. He was attached to a series of strange machines. We were constantly touching or poking or sticking him for another test. It may have been a very unpleasant experience. Many of our patients wake up confused and disoriented coming off the pump, and they've only been under anesthesia for several hours. Besides it's hard to tell what the seizures might have done."

"Agreed," Reilly answered. "Yet if he is confused, his behavior should be erratic. We should find him quickly. He's been gone only an hour. Either that or . . ."

Beeson finished his sentence, ". . . or we'll find him dead."

When I finally left the hospital, it was four in the morning and there had been no further word. I thought of going home but I could not get Jennifer out of my mind. I could still see the anguished look on her face. She would probably be fired. Yet she had seemed so innocent, so amazed at the happenings.

I decided to go see her. It was an insane hour, yet I was sure I could not sleep. Too many things were boiling over in my mind.

I found her apartment and knocked softly on her door. When there was no answer I rang the bell.

Jennifer came to the door. She looked terrible. There were large dark circles under her eyes. Her blond hair was tangled and her lipstick removed. She was obviously tired and depressed.

"Hello," she said.

"Sorry to wake you," I answered. "I had to talk with you."

She nodded and led me back into the kitchen.

"I'm glad you came by," she answered. "I wasn't having much luck sleeping. Have they found him?"

I shook my head.

"I guess I'll lose my job."

I shrugged. "Maybe not. I think Beeson is softening a little. You figure out what happened?"

She turned away and began pouring water for some coffee. "That's the funny thing," she said. "What I remember most clearly is hearing the cardiac alarm. It seemed to come out of a fog in a shrill ring. I remember being surprised to find myself down the hallway. It was like waking up from a dream, and it took me a moment to get oriented. When I reached the room all of you were there."

She looked at the floor, tears flooding into her eyes. "Boy, I really blew it. I'm so sorry, I just hope they find him."

"Beeson told me they were considering more brain surgery. The neurologists thought he was deteriorating."

"I'm not so sure," she answered. "He seemed to have periods of consciousness. Once I thought I saw him open his eyes."

"Do you think he could have been awake?"

She shrugged. "I don't know. When I think back, all I can recall is that everything seemed to be going very slowly, as if I were moving in slow motion while everything else was going at full speed. I felt as if I'd been drugged or had some terrible weights on my hands and feet. Am I making any sense?"

She stopped and wiped her eyes. "I guess it sounds like some type of flimsy excuse.

"All I can say," she added, "is that I have never left a patient in my life, and suddenly I found myself running down the hall to answer the alarm, running as fast as I could, only moving at what seemed to be half speed."

At the time I did not understand what she meant. It sounded as if she were describing some kind of altered perception. It did not occur to me to compare her description to the condition of the man they found at seven o'clock the following morning.

He was a hospital guard who had been stationed at a side door. They discovered him slumped in the garden outside the medical library. At first they thought he had suffered a stroke. He could not speak, and in his eyes was a vacant, faraway look the neurologists had never seen before. It was as if the brain had somehow been shortcircuited, the electrical connections burned out.

I went with Reilly to visit him in the hospital the next afternoon. He was kept in the locked section of the neuropsychiatric ward. The EEG which measured his brain waves showed a flat, straight line. It should be incompatible with life," the neurologists said. Yet here was a man who was alive. If you held up his arm, it remained up; if you turned his head, it did not change position. He was like a statue, incapable of any voluntary response.

Maybe just coincidence, I thought; but in the back of my mind was the growing suspicion that the guard's condition was linked to the disappearance of SUM VII. The translations of the hieroglyphic writing in the Valley of the Sphinx said the priest was capable of great feats of magic. He could "calm wild beasts" and "turn a man to stone."

19

To SAY that our attempts to capture SUM VII were doomed from the very start would be misleading, yet our hopes of finding him were based on pure conjecture. We had no idea of his whereabouts, much less if he was even alive. With every passing day we expected a call from the police or from another hospital saying that he had been found. But there was nothing.

Reilly canceled all of his classes. Beeson shut down the operating room except for emergency cases. Every spare moment was spent talking with the police, chasing leads, searching through the city streets. We worked around the clock, but there was no word, not the slightest clue.

After several days a couple visiting their father in the hospital offered a single lead. They had left the hospital late at night, and as they were driving away someone possibly fitting the Egyptian's description had darted across the street in front of them. When he was hit by the lights of their car he seemed to become scared and run. They had thought it was unusual but never bothered to report it until we started checking all people visiting the hospital the night of his disappearance. We quizzed them carefully, and their stories were conflicting: The wife said that the man had been in some type of dark clothes; the husband was not sure—perhaps there were pants but no shoes. This was the only lead we received in nearly two weeks, and it didn't take us anywhere.

By the weekend Reilly called me into his office. He had been discussing the case with Dr. Beeson. They were both concerned that SUM VII might not be found.

"Beeson thinks that he is gone for good," Reilly said, "that he may be too clever for our detection. Each day that passes increases his chance for survival. Once he learns the fundamental words like 'where?' 'food,' and 'eat,' he will seem no different than any tourist from another country. When he learns to read he will be able to keep up with the news. From then on it will be just a matter of time before our chances of finding him drop down to zero."

"Yes, but what about his medical condition," I argued. "I thought the neurologists were worried that there might be more bleeding in his brain."

"Hard to say," Reilly answered. "There's a good chance that if we find him he may not be alive. The biggest trouble then will be identifying him. Should he make it out of the state, or even out of the area, identifying him will be even more difficult. There are dozens of unclaimed bodies—displaced persons, alcoholics, murder victims—in the morgue. He could easily be lost among them. Perhaps he is lying there now. We have no way of tracing him."

I nodded slowly.

"Tell me, Bryan," Reilly said. "Say you were in a strange country and you wanted to escape. Say you were suddenly plunked back into Roman times. What would you do?"

I thought for a minute. "As long as I looked like everyone else," I said, "I would probably change my clothes and try to fit in with the rest of the population."

"Exactly," Reilly said. "And SUM VII would fit in well. He is small and he might even pass for a Latin American. As he tries to learn the language, people might assume that he can only speak Spanish and try to help him.

"And now let's look at it from our side of the fence. How do you propose that we find someone who looks like everyone else and may well be able to speak the language?"

I shrugged. "Communications. You run ads and photographs in the newspapers, alert other people to his presence. He has to come out for food. Sooner or later somebody will spot him."

"Agreed," Reilly said. "Except any publicity now might be extremely harmful to our chances. If the press got hold of this it would make the front page of every newspaper in the world. Every lunatic in the country would want his mother or his great aunt 're-suscitated' by Beeson's team. That's the last thing we need. Furthermore any untoward publicity might drive him further into hiding. I am afraid we've worked ourselves into a fine fix."

"Could we somehow lure him into the open?" I suggested.

Reilly stared at me. Suddenly his eyes flashed.

"I got it," he exclaimed.

I looked at him with bewilderment.

"Say we lured him to some neutral, nonthreatening area. Someplace like a park, or a . . ."

"A museum!" I cried. "He has to be interested in his own past. What if we lured him to a museum?"

"Bravo," Reilly answered. "We could stage a small exhibit at a museum and advertise it heavily. Tell of the priceless findings in the tomb in the Valley of the Sphinx. We could blow up some of our photographs. There are a number of museums in the area which might lend us some of their own Egyptian collections. We could start a week ahead of time—"

"Yes," I interrupted, "but again you're assuming he can read English. We don't know that at all."

"But that's what makes the plan so nice." Reilly said. "We'll write it in something I am sure he can understand."

"What do you mean?" I asked.

"Hieroglyphics, my boy." He smiled.

Two days later Reilly's secretary called me into the professor's office. He had worked up a short announcement for the paper. At the bottom were two lines of hieroglyphics.

I smiled at the sight. "But what do they say?"

"The professor copied it from one of the inscriptions in the tomb," she answered. "Abdul has recently sent us a full translation."

HERE RESTS THE HIGH PRIEST OF THE PHARAOH
KHUFU. MAY HIS SOUL SOAR FOREVER WITH
AMEN-RA.

I read the words slowly, wondering how they might
affect SUM VII. He would be reading his own epitaph.
It was a brilliant plan. Perhaps it would draw him out.
If he saw the paper. *If* he was still alive.

20

THE NEWSPAPERS ran the advertisement for an entire week. The doors to the museum would be open on Sunday from noon until five. Visitors would be permitted to walk past the Egyptian treasures, but because of the large crowd anticipated they would probably not have much chance to linger.

We hoped that the predicted size of the crowd would promise anonymity to SUM VII and encourage him to come into the open.

By the end of the week we had gathered a sizable collection of Egyptian artifacts and jewelry. Two mummies were brought up from a museum in San Jose. The burial bracelets which we had discovered on SUM VII were exhibited in a special case. Signs were made to identify each item for the visitors.

On Sunday we arrived at the museum three hours early. We went through the exhibition one final time and talked about our plan. We had a dozen guards at our disposal. It was our intention to surround the Egyptian and try to coax him to return. If this did not work, Reilly said, we would simply overpower him.

Of this second plan I was not so sure. The image of the hospital guard was still in my mind, and I did not relish the thought of spending the rest of my years in a neuropsychiatric ward. Yet it was a chance we all had to take. We had no other choice.

By noon a large crowd had gathered outside the museum, and during the first hour several hundred people filed through the doors. We initially took a station on the second floor where we could scrutinize all of the visitors. It soon became apparent that this position was inadequate. Although we could easily identify three or four people alone, the task became impossible with a crowd; finally we decided to move downstairs to a small curtained booth off the main gallery. Here, looking through an opening in the curtains, we hoped to survey the people with greater accuracy.

By three we had seen no one of particular interest. I was convinced that it was a hopeless cause, and that we had been much too optimistic from the start. Watching the endless faces hour after hour became tedious work. I soon became so tired my vision blurred. At four o'clock I told Reilly I had to go outside for some fresh air.

I walked out of the booth and casually wandered through the gallery. As I moved down the hall I studied the faces. There was a mixed lot. Some couples. Many families. Scattered teenagers. Finally I moved out of the building and stood outside. It was a typical winter day, overcast and cold.

As I returned to the center of the exhibit, I had a strange sensation similar to the feeling you have when you find someone looking at you. I stopped abruptly and looked through the crowd, but there was no one there. I started walking again but the sensation remained. Someone was watching.

It was an old woman across the hallway. A shawl covered her head. She walked stooped over, with a shuffling gait. For an instant I caught her staring at me. Then she turned and moved along with the flow of the crowd. Something about her looked strangely familiar.

I tried to catch up, but she bobbed and weaved through the people in front of me. As I pursued her, I had the odd sensation that I was moving at half speed. No matter how fast I tried to go, the distance between us remained the same.

The hallway narrowed. I could see a museum guard moving toward us. I thought about yelling out to him, but I was afraid he would think I was a fool. Certainly we had not scheduled the exhibit to capture an old woman.

Suddenly she was gone. At the same instant I

seemed able to move swiftly again. I sprinted toward
the guard, but when I reached him I could find no
trace of her. The group in which I had first seen her
caught up with us and began to proceed toward the
exit. I turned back into the museum. I was sure she
had not gone past the guard. But where was she?

A side corridor leading down one of the wings of the
museum had been roped off and was completely dark
except for a small exit light at the far end. As I stared
down the deserted hallway, a shadow passed in front of
the light.

I ran full speed down the hallway. Huge somber
portraits lined the wall. In the dim light statues that
stood along the corridor looked like real men.

Then I heard a noise. Someone was moving softly
ahead. My brow broke out in sweat. The hair on my
neck began to prickle. In the darkness my memory of
the small stooped lady became a phantom of mon-
strous proportions.

I slowed to a walk. The furnishings in the corridor
had changed. Numerous objects in glass cases lined the
walls. On the far side of them a door stood slightly
ajar. The room beyond was pitch black. I took a fal-
tering step inside.

What happened next occurred in a split second.
There was a terrible roaring sound. A screen in front
of me exploded into a motion picture as a locomotive
rushed across it. A voice came out of the darkness:

WELCOME. YOU ARE NOW VIEWING A PRO-
GRAMMED MULTI-MEDIA PRODUCTION ON THE
FAMILY OF MAN. THE PROGRESS OF CIVILIZATION
HAS BEEN ASTOUNDING. WHAT YOU ARE ABOUT TO
SEE . . .

I slammed the door shut behind me. My hands were
trembling. My throat was dry. I had thought I was
going to die. Killed by a multimedia production!

Just as I decided to go back, I heard a quick
succession of footsteps ahead. I ran after them halfheartedly. I had no desire to continue on.

I paused at a junction, trying to see into the darkness. What could have been a vague form seemed huddled in the shadows of the wall. Another statue I thought. But was it?

As I advanced slowly toward it, something brushed against my head. Reaching up along the wall my fingers came upon a long wooden object that felt like a spear. With a wrench I broke it free.

Holding the spear like a bat I advanced upon the object.

"Stop!" I cried.

At the same instant I thought the object moved. Later I could never be sure if someone had actually been there or if it was my own heightened imagination. Half in fright, half in defense, I swung the spear. As the blow gathered speed, I realized I would have only one chance. There was a dull thump as the wood struck home. Something flew out of the darkness toward me, something with terrible white teeth and huge, bug-like eyes. I tried to move but my feet were glued to the floor. There was a shuddering roar and then blackness overcame me in an onrushing wave.

21

CONSCIOUSNESS RETURNED slowly, like a small flash-light shining in the back of a dark room, always wavering and a little out of reach. I am not sure how long I was out. A voice, very faint at first, was calling my name.

"Bryan . . . Bryan, can you hear me . . . Bryan, are you all right?"

I reached up and felt something wet on my forehead. The lights in the corridor were on, and I was lying on the floor with Professor Reilly bending over me. Next to me was a huge carved mask made of heavy teakwood. Shark's teeth had been implanted in the mouth, and two shell disks were used for the eyes. At the far end of the corridor a shaft of light slanted through an exit doorway which stood ajar.

I tried to shake the grogginess from my head.

"We'd better get you to the hospital," Reilly said. "You're going to need X rays and some stitches."

I felt the damp spot again. My finger seemed to slip on something hard. My God, I thought. It was my skull. I had a huge laceration above my temple.

"What happened?" I asked.

"Mask fell on your head," Reilly said. He reached over and lifted one end. It looked as if it weighed forty pounds. "You're lucky you're still alive."

I tried to remember what I was doing in the museum, why I was there. I had been chasing someone.

The light began to fade again. As I slipped back into unconsciousness, someone said, "I think we'd better go for an ambulance."

"Well, Bryan, how are you?" Professor Reilly said in his office the next afternoon. He seemed quite pleased that I was up and about. I was pleased just to be alive.

"All right, I guess," I answered. "Any more news?"

Reilly shook his head. "You remember any more of it now?"

I thought for a moment. The truth was that I remembered even less than I had before.

"In the hospital you told us about the woman. About the men's shoes. About chasing someone through the darkened corridor."

I winced, trying to piece the faint fragments together. When I tried to think, I could only feel the throbbing in my forehead.

"It may well have been SUM VII." Reilly nodded.

"Hmmph," I grunted. "Sorry I let him get away."

"Well, you made a big dent in the side of a ceremonial mask."

"That's some consolation." I tried to smile.

"You also made a sizable dent in a carved wooden idol which was standing in the corner." Reilly leaned back in his chair, placing his hands behind his head. "We were awfully close to him that time. I doubt if we'll fool him again."

"Well, at least we know he is in the area," I offered.

"Or was," Reilly answered. "If it was SUM VII, he had a very close call."

I rubbed the side of my head. "Not to mention me."

"Think you're well enough to go back to work?" he asked.

"If you mean in the hospital, I have to present a case tomorrow on rounds."

"And today?"

"They were nice and gave me the afternoon off," I answered. "It was only a concussion. No brain oozing out."

"Good," Reilly said. His mind was already contemplating something else. "We got a call from the language lab. Apparently they made some progress with the translations."

"That's good news!" I exclaimed. I was beginning to forget my headache. "You want me to check it out?"

"If you think you're up to it. If not I'll get over there first thing in the morning."

I stood up. "I can go over right now."

He nodded, shuffling through some papers on his desk. Finally he found what he was searching for, a short typed letter from a commercial isotope laboratory.

"Maybe the language lab can help clear up some of the confusion in this dating process."

Shortly after the unwrapping we had sent some bone samples of SUM VII to an isotope laboratory for radiocarbon dating. In the past this had proved a reliable method for dating Egyptian finds. "All of the bone fragments from the baboon came out exactly as we had predicted," Reilly said. "2700 B.C., give or take a few hundred years. These are approximate dates for the building of the Great Pyramid. We obtained similar dates for bits of wood from the sarcophagus of SUM VII and for some wood fragments found in the burial chambers."*

But this was not news. The translation of the "Letter to the Dead" which Abdul had sent, the references in the hieroglyphics on the walls of the tomb, the historical dating of the Great Pyramid, all placed SUM VII in that approximate era. In fact a carbon dating for SUM VII of less then 4,500 years would have been highly suspicious. Yet I was hardly prepared for what Reilly was to tell me next. He held a small graph in his hand. "There is one large concentration of radioactive carbon," he said, "that dates out at approximately 27,000 years. It's from the bone fragments of SUM VII."

I coughed and tried to clear my throat. "You think there's something wrong with the date?"

"We've checked it three times."

"There's got to be a laboratory error," I said.

* Radiocarbon dating techniques utilize the fact that all living organisms (both plant and animal) absorb a fixed amount of carbon-14 from the atmosphere. When the organism dies, the carbon-14 disintegrates at a predicted rate of decay. By measuring the amount of carbon-14 which remains in the sample, one can calcuate the approximate age. The technique is roughly accurate to 70,000 years.

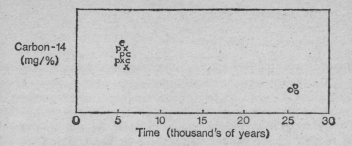

Figure 5. Radiocarbon dating SUM VII, Stanford Radioisotope Lab

Key: c = wood from casket (SUM VII)
         p = bone fragments SUM VI (baboon)
         o = skin sample SUM VII (Egyptian)
         x = wood from casket (SUM VII)

"The lab denies it. They've run it through with their controls. They keep coming up with the same figure: 27,000 years."

"But that's impossible!" I protested. "For one thing that would place him in prehistory, far before the first known writing. Besides we know that he was buried at the approximate time of Khufu."

"True. Very true," Reilly answered. "But say he lived 27,000 years ago. Perhaps the Egyptians somehow found the body and merely buried it again."

"Impossible!" I shook my head. "Too many of our references indicate that he was alive at the time of Khufu. He obviously knows and can read hieroglyphics. The carbon dating has to be wrong."

"Agreed," Reilly said. "It doesn't make any sense. Yet look at our latest results. When the laboratory sent back the first samples, I submitted others. The findings still came out the same."

I shook my head again. "It defies all scientific reasoning. You don't believe it, do you?"

He looked at me out of the corner of his eye. "No, of course not," he answered. Yet somehow his response was not convincing. It seemed to be what he thought he should say rather than what he really believed.

22

My HEAD had barely begun to clear by the time I reached the computer language lab. We couldn't ignore the consistency and reproducibility of the carbon-14 findings, but there was no logical explanation for them. Some theory that could explain SUM VII's age had to exist. The problem could be accepted only as another inexplicable facet of SUM VII.

Inside the laboratory Mr. Spanzerelli was still working on the BABEL program. When I found him, he was watching a series of Japanese characters dance across a display screen, his hair as unkempt as ever. He glanced up as I approached, his eyes slowly rolling into focus.

"My goodness," he exclaimed. "What happened to you?"

"Ran into a door," I answered, trying to smile.

"Tough," he said. "Professor Reilly send you over?"

"He told me you had some results."

"Yes, indeed," he answered. He rubbed his hands together in excitement. The translation of languages obviously delighted him.

He stood up from his chair and led me over to a small cubicle that contained headphones, a console, and a display screen. Here we could listen to the tape without disturbing the rest of the room.

As I put on a pair of headphones, Spanzerelli began punching in a number of signals to the computer. Lights began to flash, tapes whirred, and words appeared on the screen.

BABEL DISPLAY. SOUND MODE. TAPES SUM VII.
EGYPTIAN.

He punched another key and a second line read:

TRANSLATE.

A foreign language filled the headphones. I listened for a moment before realizing that it sounded Oriental and familiar. It was Japanese!

Spanzerelli looked at me, a sheepish grin on his face.

"Sorry," he said. "I forgot to punch out the Japanese mode on the other program."

He started again, repeating the instruction on the keyboard.

BABEL DISPLAY. SOUND MODE. TAPES SUM VII.
EGYPTIAN/ENGLISH.

The tape spun crazily before stopping with a click, to be followed by a constant droning that lasted nearly ten seconds. Then SUM VII's voice came over the headphones in English, mimicking a conversation between Reilly and Beeson.

"I think my watch has stopped," the voice said. "What time do you have?"

"One thirty-five . . . but that can't be right . . ."

Both sides of the dialogue were repeated without changing inflection. I remembered how amazed I had been when I heard SUM VII do this.

Spanzerelli shut off the machine. "It's an incredible thing," he said. "His mind has perfect retention, almost like a tape itself."

He pushed a series of buttons on the console, and after some high-pitched chatter SUM VII came on again, but his words were unrecognizable. He rattled on for a few minutes before stopping. A low moan rose in the background as SUM VII drifted back into unconsciousness. A nurse called for medication. Spanzerelli stopped the tape.

"We have listened to all six hours of the recording," he said. "There are several long periods in which nothing was said. Other times it seems as if he's lost his train of thought. We have been able to identify three distinctly different types of speech. The first one, at the beginning of the tape, is English and, as you heard, was merely a repetition of words that SUM VII learned in the hospital. The second type of speech, which you've just now heard, is Egyptian, or very early Arabic, the language he used during the middle of his delirium. The third type of speech is a language that we have never heard before.

"For a long time we tried to translate the Egyptian portion without results. The funny thing is that I kept thinking there was something wrong with the computer. Then suddenly it became ridiculously clear. What he was doing for part of the time was repeating the English conversation, only he had translated it into Egyptian. And this was our key! Once we understood this, we were able to get on the right track. The position of the words in the sentences, the placement of the verbs, the nouns, the adjectives could now be identified, and the rest of what he said in Egyptian opened up. We typed in hieroglyphic readings so that we could program the phonetic pronunciation of the words. It took us fifteen more computer hours, but we finally got it."

I was amazed. Who knows how long such a feat would have taken without the computer. Probably it would have been impossible. No human could store the words from a number of languages, sort them out, and spit them back in seconds the way a computer could. No one, I thought, except perhaps SUM VII.

"Now," Spanzerelli said, "we have been able to put together five passages of the Egyptian that have nothing to do with translations of what he said in English. You can take a copy back. I hope Reilly will be pleased."

"He'll be delighted," I said excitedly. My own interest had been raised to a keen pitch. I could hardly wait to read the translations from the Egyptian. What secrets did they hold? What key did they uncover to SUM VII's past?

Spanzerelli dug into a file cabinet and pulled out a thin manilla folder, spreading the contents across a desk. At first I was disappointed. I had wished for

great volumes of translated material, for words and
passages which gave the history of SUM VII, episodes
from his life, keys to his past. Yet the entire printout
consisted of only four pages. And some of these appeared to have no meaning at all.

As I read them I could hear SUM VII's voice, rich,
and distinct, behind them.

PASSAGE I. BABEL PROGRAM. EGYPTIAN/ENGLISH
TRANSLATION. SUM VII. PRINT MODE. PRINT ENG-
LISH.

WE HAVE ONE CHOICE. IF WE STICK TOGETHER
THERE IS A CHANCE THAT NONE OF US WILL SUR-
VIVE. IF WE SPLIT THEN THERE IS A CHANCE
THAT ONE MAYBE TWO OF US CAN MAKE IT OUT.
WE MUST GET BACK. WE MUST FIND THE PEOPLE.
AS KING OF . . .

REJECT, COMPUTER ERROR. WORD "KING" ENG-
LISH. ERROR. CORRECT TRANSLATION ARABIC/
EGYPTIAN TO ENGLISH EQUIVALENT: LEADER,
CAPTAIN. OMIT "KING." SUBSTITUTE "CAPTAIN."

READOUT CONTINUED: . . . AS CAPTAIN OF THIS
SHIP I WILL TAKE FULL RESPONSIBILITY. DAR-
TANE WILL GO TO THE SOUTH. REDIPTION, YOU,
TO THE NORTH. I WILL TAKE THE EAST. BAR-
TAGNIA, YOU, THE WEST. . . . WE HAVE NO OTHER
CHOICE. . . . LET THE FIRST OF YOU THAT MAKES
IT TRY TO CONTACT THE PEOPLE. . . . IT IS OUR
ONLY HOPE. . . . IF WE ARE TO SURVIVE. . . . IF
ANY OF US WILL LIVE TO SEE THE PORT AGAIN
WE MUST DO THIS. . . . OTHERWISE WE WILL PER-
ISH . . . OUR FATE . . . OUR TERRIBLE FATE. . . .
OUR DESTINY . . .

COMPUTER TRANSLATION: "DARTANE" (PROPER
NAME, NO ENGLISH EQUIVALENT). "REDIPTION"
(PROPER NAME NO ENGLISH EQUIVALENT). "BAR-
TAGNIA" (PROPER NAME, NO ENGLISH EQUIVA-
LENT).

COMPUTER TRANSLATION: "PORT": NO KNOWN
ENGLISH EQUIVALENT. POSSIBLE ALTERNATE

TRANSLATION: BODY, SPHERE, HOME. POSSIBLY PLANET, SUN, STAR. CONNOTATION CHECK: "PORT" SATISFACTORY WITH MEANING OF SENTENCE. KEY WORDS: "SHIP"; "TRAVEL"; "CAPTAIN."

When I finished reading the passage I looked questioningly at Spanzerelli. "I don't understand it."

Spanzerelli shrugged. "We're just here to provide the translation."

"And you're sure it's right?"

He nodded slowly. "Let's just say that it's unlikely the computer is wrong."

What was SUM VII talking about? There was no question that he was speaking in earnest, but whether he was recalling a specific conversation or merely hallucinating, it was impossible to tell.

I turned to the second passage.

PASSAGE II. BABEL PROGRAM. EGYPTIAN/ENGLISH TRANSLATION. SUM VII. PRINT MODE. PRINT ENGLISH.

THE STRUCTURE SHOULD STAND BEST IF WE SET THE CORNER STONES IN EACH OF THE FOUR DIRECTIONS, FACING EXACTLY EAST, WEST, NORTH, AND SOUTH. I WOULD RECOMMEND A DESCENDING PASSAGE AT A SLOPE OF FOURTEEN DEGREES FROM THE NORTH FACE LEADING INTO THE CENTRAL CORE. FOR THE DOOR WE CAN CONSTRUCT A SWINGING OPENING WHICH WILL BE INVISIBLE FROM THE OUTSIDE.

HAVE CALCULATED THE DIMENSION AT 746 CUBITS. THE INNER PASSAGES SHOULD BE CONSTRUCTED AS THE HEIGHT OF THE BUILDING COMMENCES AND I NOW HAVE AN IDEA TO SEAL THE INNERMOST ASCENDING PASSAGE LEADING UP TO THE MAIN CHAMBER.

I read the passage with scarcely a breath. Here was proof of our theory that SUM VII had a very large role in the building and construction of the Great Pyramid. In fact this conversation made him appear instrumental in the original design!

But the next passage was as disappointing as the first. The translation was imperfect and the text seemed of little consequence.

PASSAGE III. BABEL PROGRAM. EGYPTIAN/ENGLISH TRANSLATION. SUM VII. PRINT MODE. PRINT ENGLISH.

THOU ART THE GREAT STAR, THE COMPANION OF SETH WHO CROSSES THE SKY, WHO TRAVELS OVER THE LAKES OF THE DANCERS. OSIRIS, IT IS YOU WHO ASCENDEST IN THE EASTERN SKY, RENEWED IN THY TIME, REJUVENATED IN THY HOUR. NUT WAS BORN TO THEE, THE DANCE COMES DOWN TO THEE. A MEAL IS GIVEN TO THEE, THE PRIEST LAMENTS FOR THEE AS FOR OSIRIS IN HIS SUFFERING.

The words could have been some type of religious utterance that SUM VII might have said as a priest.

The fourth passage proved of little more value than the third.

PASSAGE IV. BABEL PROGRAM. EGYPTIAN/ENGLISH TRANSLATION. SUM VII. PRINT MODE. PRINT ENGLISH.

HIGH OVER THE EARTH, THOU ART ABOVE THE FATHER WHO HAS MASTERY OVER HIM. HE IS LOVED IN THAT HE HAS SET HIMSELF UNDER ALL THE THINGS THAT ARE THINE. THOU HAST TAKEN THE GREAT GOD TO THYSELF WITH HIS BOAT, THOU HAST EDUCATED THEM AS A THOUSAND SOULS SO THAT THEY WILL NOT DISAPPEAR FROM THE STARS. . . .

The fifth and final passage was briefer than any of the other four. It contained more word fragments and fewer sentences and may have been spoken as SUM VII drifted into the deepest portion of his delirium.

PASSAGE V. BABEL PROGRAM. EGYPTIAN/ENGLISH
TRANSLATION. SUM VII. PRINT MODE. PRINT ENG-
LISH.

MUST GET BACK. . . . MUST NOT GET TRAPPED.
. . . THERE MUST BE SOME WAY . . . SOME
WAY TO . . . RETURN. . . .

However fragmented the words the emotion behind
them was unmistakable. Spanzerelli played this section
of the tape for me. SUM VII's voice was hoarse and
strained.

"There are five or six other passages," Spanzerelli
said. "I'll play one of them for you. Together they
compose the third distinct language on the tapes."

The voice that came over the headphones was indeed speaking a strange language. The words were
short, almost musical in quality, and like no other language I had ever heard. I was not sure it was even
SUM VII's voice.

As we listened, the words became more forced, the
tone more gasping and urgent. The voice rose. Repeated itself. Then there was silence. Nothing was
said for another five minutes until, softly, like a window shutter flapping in the breeze, a faint thumping
sound came on, followed by a nurse saying, "He's
having another seizure. We'll need more medication."

Spanzerelli reached forward and turned off the tape.
"He must have become unconscious again," he said.
"That's all there is."

23

WHEN I arrived back at the anatomy lab, Reilly's secretary informed me that he had had to leave to attend an urgent meeting with the dean. I handed her the stack of computer translations and started to go.

"He asked if you might join them," she said.

"Do you know what it's about?"

"I'm not sure," she answered. "The dean was very excited. He called Professor Reilly out of the middle of a lecture and told him to dismiss his class."

Calling a professor out of class meant that something very important was up. The fact that I had been invited indicated it had to do with SUM VII. There could be no other reason.

I thanked Ms. Jacobson and hurried out of the door. Had they found SUM VII? The prospect that even now he might be resting in the safety of the hospital elated me, and halfway across the campus I broke into a run. But when I reached the dean's office, the room was deserted. There was no secretary, no student assistants, none of the usual personnel.

At the end of the corridor was a conference room. I could hear muffled voices inside and I quietly opened the door. The room was dark. A large slide was projected upon a screen. A man standing in front of a lectern was speaking about the structure of blood. Then I recognized Dean Chapman sitting next to the wall. The dean motioned me inside. Next to him, I could make out Dr. Reilly and Dr. Beeson, the latter still dressed in a surgical mask and gown. Others from the faculty and the staff were also present. The speaker was a physician named P.J. Smythe, a tall, thin man with a deep voice and a receding chin, who had a special interest in the molecular constituents of blood.

"We, of course, were quite eager to measure the hemoglobin of the Egyptian," Smythe was saying, "especially since we have had no actual recording of blood states which existed during that time, other than rough blood typing from tissue samples of various mummies.

"The first electrophoretic pattern of SUM VII showed predominately hemoglobin Type A. This sample was drawn the second day while the Egyptian was still in Intensive Care. A second and third sample were taken a week and two weeks later, and then a fourth sample at the end of the twenty-first day.

"Most unusual is the fact that the hemoglobin A pattern begins to disappear and is finally replaced by a new hemoglobin molecule which has a migration pattern different from any other hemoglobin we have seen. We were at a loss to explain this until we realized that at first most of his blood came from the extracorporeal pump. This was 'priming' blood and not his own. As time passed he began manufacturing his own red cells. This is the change we began to see with the electrophoresis."

Smythe now changed the slide. The new photograph was a schematic drawing of the hemoglobin molecule.

"Now, gentlemen," he began, "what I am going to tell you is a scientific discovery that I cannot explain. I can merely tell you what we found. In our laboratories these past few days we have begun to investigate the molecule of hemoglobin which the Egyptian was manufacturing in his own bone marrow. We know that it migrated at a much different rate from other known hemoglobins. We know that the red cells have a much longer survival time than normal red cells. Yet we could not understand why.

"Yesterday we identified the difference. It is a small, very tiny change, but one of immense importance, because it involves the position on the hemoglobin chain in which certain amino acid abnormalities occur. Yet the substituted compound is not an amino acid at all. In fact it is not a compound which naturally occurs in man or any other form of mammals that we know.

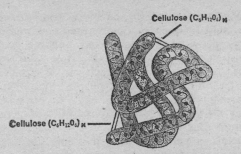

Figure 6. Three-dimensional tertiary structure of the protein hemoglobin of SUM VII, showing cellulose binding sites. Taken from schematic drawing. P.J. Smythe, Dept. of Pathology, University Medical Center.

It is cellulose, a compound fround predominately in plants."

A loud murmur swept the room. There were a dozen questions, everyone speaking at the same time. Smythe turned on the lights and paused in front of the lectern to light a pipe. A fine sheen of perspiration glistened on his brow.

"One at a time, please," he said.

"Do you have any theories?" a woman asked.

Smythe shrugged. "Perhaps one can explain it with genetic manipulation. It's possible that one could prepare a body or a person for long-term survival by substituting certain genetic differences into the system. There are a variety of spores, or viruses, of various forms of plant life which can withstand tremendously long periods of inactivity and extremes in temperature. Why does a bristle pine live for three thousand years and a shrew for less than a year? These are things which are inherent to the organism through its genetic endowment.

"We know that the Egyptian was able to heal a long bone fracture in a single week. Certain plants can heal fractures of a stem in several days. Bamboo can grow six inches in a twenty-four-hour period.

"Again this is just a theory, but I think that the

precise placement of the cellulose compound in the amino acid sequences gives the compound great strength, provides a cross-linked bonding which the normal hemoglobin molecule does not have. In plants cellulose is the substance which makes up the tough outer stem. This may be its purpose here, only on a molecular level."

"Why do you suggest the possibility of genetic engineering?" Beeson asked.

"Because a genetic mutation seems far less likely, and I think we would have seen evidence of it in other humans. Mutations which survive are usually very small changes on a molecular level. Over a course of hundreds of thousands of years they gradually take hold and alter the evolutionary path."

"You speak of such things as genetic engineering, yet we are dealing with a man who lived five thousand years ago," Beeson argued. "There is little evidence to indicate a civilization capable of such a feat existing then."

Smythe smiled. "You are correct, sir. I can only tell you what I have found. I am reporting the facts, not the explanation. Someone asked me for a theory and I offered one."

"Where do you propose we go from here?" Dean Chapman asked.

"We need to do much more experimental work. We need more blood, more samples, more tissue specimens, more everything. In short we need the Egyptian."

"Has there been any progress in locating him?"

Smythe shrugged. "That is not my department," he said. He looked over at Dr. Reilly.

"Negative," Reilly answered.

"And there is no knowledge of his whereabouts?"

"Absolutely none."

"And what is your hope now?"

"If you mean of finding him alive, poor," Reilly answered. "Each day that passes increases the chances that his aneurysm may break loose. The neurologist gave him only several weeks."

A gentleman with a beard and a white coat stood up slowly. "There is one thing I cannot understand," he said. "On the one hand you are concerned about this man bleeding further into the brain, possibly dying, and on the other hand you tell us that he has certain molecular substitutions which enable his cells to maintain almost indefinite life. Aren't these two things incompatible?"

"Not necessarily," Smythe responded. "The living organism, as we understand it, maintains a very delicate balance of nutrients, oxygen, and electrolytes. Once this balance stops, as it would with a disruption in the circulation, all of the cells begin to degenerate and die. With the Egyptian this does not seem to be the case. If he suffers a major disruption in his brain, his general functions will stop, but the organs themselves may survive.

"It's like your car. You get a hole in the gasoline line and it stops running. Yet the headlights, the radiator, the fuel pump remain intact."

"Then he is capable of death?"

"It is a matter of definition," Smythe answered. "If you mean ceasing function, yes."

At the end of the conference I followed Reilly out of the room. The computer translations seemed of little importance now. I had never seen him quite so depressed.

When I caught up with him his head was cast downward, his eyes staring toward the ground. "Bryan, there is one other thing I think we must do," he said slowly. "I have thought about it a hundred times," he said, "wondering how to tell him. I kept hoping that we could bring everything together without him, but perhaps I've been wrong. He may be the one key that's been missing, the one person who can help us more than anyone else. If we needed him before, I am afraid we need him most desperately now."

"Who is that?" I asked.

He turned toward me, but even before he answered I realized whom he was referring to. It was the man with a face tanned by a thousand Egyptian suns, the huge man who had led us across the desert in search of the Valley of the Sphinx, the man who stood like a shadow against the backdrop of the great pyramids in the photograph with the caption: "Man Seeking Man."

It was Abdul.

24

By MIDNIGHT a cable of utmost urgency sped its way toward a destination halfway around the world.

ANTIQUITIES DEPARTMENT
MINISTRY OF CULTURE
UNITED ARAB REPUBLIC
CAIRO

REQUEST URGENT ASSISTANCE FROM ABDUL MUHAMMAD EL-SADIR IN MEDICAL RESEARCH EGYPTIAN PROJECT SUM VII STOP TRANSPORTATION AND LODGING COVERED BY UNIVERSITY FUNDING GRANT 17450-D STOP REQUEST IMMEDIATE DEPARTURE STOP CABLE FLIGHT AND ARRIVAL TIME FOR SAN FRANCISCO

> PROFESSOR J ARNOLD REILLY
> DEPARTMENT OF ANATOMY
> UNIVERSITY MEDICAL CENTER

Seventy-two hours later a Boeing 747 taxied up to the main terminal at the San Francisco International Airport. I searched eagerly through the passengers. Abdul was the last man to get off the plane, bending over to squeeze his huge frame through the door.

"Greetings, Mr. St. John," he said. I shook his hand warmly, remembering when I had stepped off the plane in Cairo with the heat waves shimmering off the runway. Abdul had been there to meet me, snatching my luggage with a single sweep of his massive arm. Looking at him I had a renewed sense that maybe everything would turn out all right. The old team was back together again.

That afternoon we met at the professor's house for

tea. Reilly had corresponded extensively with Abdul over the previous months. Now he reviewed the entire story, detail by detail. Abdul stood like a stone, his arms folded. As he listened to Reilly describe our attempts to communicate with SUM VII through hieroglyphics, his eyes moistened, and his lips drew taut. Except for this single moment no other expression crossed his face.

When Reilly finished, Abdul nodded slowly.

"That which you ask me to do is not easy," he said. "This is not my country."

"I know," Reilly answered. "I am afraid this is the toughest assignment I've ever given you. But I thought you, more than anyone, might have some idea of what he would do once he left the hospital."

Abdul frowned. "What do you have to go on?"

"Nothing," Reilly answered. "Absolutely nothing. Only that he is Egyptian. That he was most probably a high priest. That he seems capable of unusual mental phenomena. And that perhaps now he speaks some English."

Listening to the professor Abdul stood very still, gazing silently across the room. "I think two things," he finally said. "First that he has not gone very far. The Egyptian way in old times was to travel on foot, and I am thinking that he would not have changed. Second that he must be assisted by someone who brings him food and clothing. He may be very clever, but without some help I do not think he could have survived. One final thing. If the museum where Mr. St. John was injured is near the hospital, if it is easily reached on foot, then we must search within this radius."

He shrugged. "These are humble opinions," he said. "I am sorry that I cannot offer you more."

Before we broke from tea that afternoon, Abdul and the professor had pored over maps of the campus and the surrounding grounds, noting that the museum was only five miles' distance. On the other side of the medical center were rolling hills which drifted off into the Santa Cruz Mountains. And it was from these hills that we obtained our first real lead, although the way it came about took us completely by surprise.

Seven days after P. J. Smythe's announcement of the abnormal hemoglobin Professor Reilly received a handwritten note in the mail. It was addressed to the hospital and had been opened by the department of administration before being forwarded.

Dear Sir,

     I was at the hospital last week when you was looking for a patient that escaped. I want to let you know I seen a man in a cabin here near the observatory. He has been making funny pictures. If you are interested and there is a reward, contact me at once.

                    Sincerely,
                    Joseph Hawkins
                    1032 Skyline Drive

Reilly's first reaction was that the letter was a hoax, but when we looked up the address, Skyline Drive proved to be a small winding road which crossed a long ridge next to the university observatory. It was a remote section of the campus, one we had not fully explored. I told Reilly I would check it out.

Skyline Drive curved and twisted up into the mountains. Patches of forest crept down along the ridges while below the land curved off into gentle fields. At the top of a long rise the road passed the gate to the university observatory. Here a complex of buildings housed one of the world's largest reflecting telescopes. A huge dome towered above the buildings.

A quarter of a mile away Hawkins address was listed on a rusted mailbox half-hidden from the road. A dirt driveway led back to an old farmhouse surrounded by trees. I was greeted by the loud barking of a dozen dogs, but no one was there. The house was boarded and closed.

I drove back to the observatory and stopped at the gate. I showed the guard Joseph Hawkins' letter. "Mr.

Hawkins was one of our semiretired caretakers," he said. "He lived on this property for the past fifty years. You're going to have a tough time talking to him, though."

"How's that?"

"His health was poor. They found him the other day unconscious."

"Unconscious?" I latched on to the word. Had yet another man been rendered mute by SUM VII?

"And the cabin that he referred to? Do you know where it is?"

"Might be the old caretaker's house," the guard said. "Was used for a while when they were building the observatory a dozen years ago."

He pointed across a steep valley. Nestled in the corner of a thick clump of trees, partially obscured, was the outline of a shack. I nodded, my mind racing. A remote section of the campus. A small isolated cabin. An old man found unconscious. Maybe I was on to something. I thought about calling Reilly, but rejected the idea. My evidence was still flimsy at best.

"Anybody live there now?" I asked.

The guard shook his head. "Been nobody there for several years."

"Can I drive over to it?"

"Road's not good," he said. "If you got four-wheel drive you can make it, but I wouldn't advise it. There's a path you can walk pretty easily. The college kids hike past it sometimes."

I left the car and traveled on foot. The pathway led across the valley and down to a section of dense woods where I found the cabin. The windows were broken, the roof shabby. If someone wanted a place to hide, it would have been a perfect spot.

I knocked on the door. When there was no answer I gave it a little push. To my surprise it swung slowly open.

From the broken-down appearance of the cabin I had imagined the inside would be full of scattered debris. Instead it was neat and the floor cleanly swept. A small bed with a mattress and a folded blanket occupied one corner. Next to the bed was a simple desk and a light.

I walked over to the bed and looked underneath. Nothing there. Then I opened the closet. There were three simple hangers. On two were men's shirts and a pair of pants. On the other was a woman's sweater and a shawl.

As I closed the closet door, it hit me. The old woman in the museum had been wearing a similar kind of shawl!

I searched the cabin again. In the corner of the room underneath the desk I found a stack of neatly folded newspapers. I pulled them out, and stuck away in the middle of them was a writing tablet filled with sheets of figures that represented some form of higher mathematics. One page showed a long circular line which appeared to be an orbit or an ellipse. Sketched coordinates below it were followed by more calculations. And in the bottom right-hand corner were three small hieroglyphs. They could only have been drawn by the Egyptian.

No sooner did I realize that I had found the hiding place of SUM VII than panic overtook me. What if SUM VII discovered me in the cabin? I could still remember the expression on the guard's face in the neuropsychiatric ward. And now, Mr. Hawkins, the man who wrote us the letter, was also unconscious in the hospital. I had little hope of surviving a similar encounter. The chase in the museum had been close enough.

I considered taking one of the sheets of strange calculations, but decided I should leave everything exactly as I had found it. Not the slightest hint should arouse his suspicion. I piled the papers neatly and put them back where I had found them. At the same moment a twig cracked outside. I froze instantly. Slow, plodding footsteps were coming toward the cabin!

With a leap I crossed the floor and wedged myself inside the closet. The cabin door opened, and a floorboard creaked as someone entered. Footsteps moved, then stopped, then moved toward the closet.

I readied myself. I knew I would get one chance and that was all.

Perhaps I could catch him by surprise.

The footsteps stopped outside the closet door, and very slowly the door began to move! With a desperate kick I rammed it open.

The sudden scream made my hair stand on end.

"My God!" I gasped, for I was little prepared for the sight in front of me.

25

WE STARED at each other, and as I looked at the attractive blond girl who stood before me, some of the pieces of the puzzle began to fit together.

"Jennifer," I stammered, "but how? Why?"

She quickly regained her composure. "Bryan, what are you doing here?" she asked angrily.

"What are you doing here?" I answered. "Then it was you who have brought him food and clothing. It is you who have helped him."

She nodded slowly.

"But we've got to get him back to the hospital."

"For what?" she answered angrily. "So that he can have more tests, so that he can have another operation. He's kept like some captive animal over there."

She bowed her head, her eyes suddenly filling with tears. "Bryan, please," she pleaded. "Don't turn him in. He's not hurting anyone. Just leave him alone for a few more days."

"But why?" I answered.

"Don't you see?" she cried. "Don't you see that he is dying?"

"Then we should get him back . . ."

"No, no," she interrupted. "Do this one thing for me. Leave now. I'll meet you in the hospital later. If he finds you here, there will be trouble. Believe me. I can explain everything. But not now. Get out before he returns."

I could tell from the expression in her eyes how desperate she was. I was torn between wanting to trust her and the knowledge that she had deceived us.

"All right," I finally said. "Meet me this afternoon at the hospital, four o'clock in the cafeteria. I'll keep everything quiet. But only if you agree to tell me the entire story. If you're not there by four, I'll bring everyone to the cabin."

She nodded without speaking.

What more could I say? I wanted to dash back to the lab and tell Reilly everything. Instead I was involving myself as deeply as Jennifer.

"And you," I asked, "are you sure you'll be all right?"

"Don't worry about me," she said. "Just go. I'll meet you later."

That afternoon I went to the hospital early. Mr. Hawkins, the caretaker, was in a coma in Intensive Care. I reviewed his chart. For years he had suffered from high blood pressure. He had been hospitalized for two small strokes before. Perhaps SUM VII had not harmed him at all.

When I went to the hospital cafeteria, Jennifer was already there, looking worried and tired. I bought her coffee and we sat down.

"Start at the beginning," I said. "The night you told me that you had felt the altered perception, that everything was going in slow motion. That was all a lie?"

"No, no." She shook her head. "That was all the truth."

"Then what happened?"

"I don't know how he escaped that night," she said. "Everything I told you was true. I was working by his bedside. I was only gone for a couple of minutes when the cardiac alarm rang. By the time I returned he'd vanished."

"But why did he need to escape?"

"I'm not sure," she said.

"Do you communicate with him?"

"In a funny sort of way," she answered. "He speaks English very poorly, I think mostly because he hasn't tried. We seem to communicate by telepathy, or whatever you call it. Two or three days after his disappearance I went up into the fields, sure I was going to lose my job. I was near the cabin. I passed it three times before I went up to the door. And then I found him. I think somehow he had sent a signal for me to come. He was lying in the bed, half-dead. He must have discovered the cabin and stumbled inside. I had taken care of him so much in the hospital that it seemed natural to continue there. He obviously trusted me. You remember the time he placed my finger in his mouth and stopped the bleeding. I don't think I was ever really afraid."

"Did he hurt you in any way?"

"No," she answered. "At first he merely wanted food and water. They were easy enough to bring. Then he managed to make me understand he wanted clothing. He had found an old pair of pants and a shirt.

"As he grew stronger," she continued, "he began foraging on his own. His needs are small, and he eats little. Mostly vegetables and certain green and leafy plants."

Another link of the chain fell into place. The cellulose on the hemoglobin molecule. He needed vegetable and plant matter to survive.

"How often did you go to the cabin?" I asked.

"Almost every day," she answered.

"And no one discovered you?"

"Only once," she said. "An old man came snooping around. I think he worked for the observatory. I saw him leaving when I arrived. Apparently he didn't take anything. The Egyptian wasn't there. For a day or so I was afraid the man would come back. But I never saw him again."

I stopped Jennifer and showed her the letter from Joseph Hawkins.

She read it slowly. "I guess we couldn't have stayed there much longer," she said.

"Christ," I answered, "you had half the university looking for you. I'm surprised you weren't discovered long ago."

Pain filled her eyes. "Oh, Bryan, I tried to tell you a dozen times. I knew you were searching for him. I . . . I . . . I just couldn't. He seemed so lonesome, so helpless."

I nodded. "But what about the women's clothing in the closet?"

"Oh, that," she answered sheepishly. "He pointed out some women's clothes to me one day in the paper. I brought him a sweater and a shawl. I wasn't sure why he wanted them."

"Does he read much?"

"He can't read English, of course, but he liked to look at the pictures in the newspaper. Once he showed me some hieroglyphic writing in an advertisement for an exhibition in the museum. He was quite excited about it."

"What about all the calculations on the pages in the cabin? What is that all about?"

She shook her head.

"Jennifer," I said firmly, "I think we should bring him back to the hospital."

"Bryan, can't you understand?" she cried. "I'm not sure he'll last another couple of days."

"What do you mean?" I frowned.

"I mean that he is becoming progressively paralyzed. He can no longer use his right arm."

"Good Lord!" I exclaimed. "That is all the more reason to bring him back. The aneurysm must be leaking. He will need another operation."

"The odds of his making it through another operation are very low," she said. "He's not some guinea pig—some experimental animal."

"Yes, but at least he has a chance."

"A chance for what?"

"To live," I answered angrily. But my words sounded hollow. Suddenly I wondered if we were right to hunt him down like an escaped animal. I looked at Jennifer. What had started out as anger had turned into admiration. She had taken great risks to care for him and had stood up for what she believed in.

"Don't you think he has a right to choose for himself?" she said. "Maybe he doesn't want to go back to the hospital. Maybe he wants to die with dignity. Why can't he be free to make his own choice?"

"Maybe if he was like you or me," I protested, "he should have the right. But he is different. Man may never again have access to the knowledge he can provide. We have got to give him a chance."

"Chance for what?" she answered angrily. "Chance for one more experimental operation with little hope for success."

"Yes," I answered firmly. "Absolutely. If there is some hope of life for him, if there is some hope that he can survive, it will all have been worthwhile. There are so many beautiful things in this world. Simple things. A tree, a flower, a cloud. Life is so much better than death. Death is nothing."

By this time I was practically shouting. Half the people in the cafeteria were looking at us.

"Maybe he has to go through another operation," I yelled, "but he's come this far. We can't abandon him now.

"Come on." I stood up and grabbed her hand. "We're going over to see Dr. Reilly. I'm sure it's the right thing to do."

I placed my arm around her shoulders and led her out of the cafeteria. For the first time since we had lost SUM VII, I was absolutely sure I was right.

I called the professor to tell him we were coming. We met at his home. When we arrived he led us into the study. Abdul stood in the corner, silently watching.

Reilly asked Jennifer to sit down. When she had finished telling her story, he turned to Abdul.

"What do you think?" he said.

The huge Egyptian folded his arms in front of him.

"There is an old saying in our country. 'A man's last travels should be downstream.' All of my training says that we should go and bring him back. But the Egyptian inside me says we are going against the current. Perhaps we should let him die in peace."

Abdul had come halfway across the world to help us, spending hours covering a myraid of leads. Now he was willing to give the whole thing up. I was completely taken aback by his answer. Reilly looked at him with concern. He, too, was surprised.

"You are telling me that you would not have approved the resuscitation?"

Abdul bowed. "Sir, you did not seek my advice."

Reilly turned toward me. "Bryan?"

I stood up slowly, torn by a dozen emotions. "In all respect," I finally said, "I disagree. I think we should bring him back. If he is dying, I think we should at least offer him a chance. There is still hope. We have learned much even though it may have been at his expense. The circumstances are different now. We could go more slowly. Perhaps ultimately he could go back to Egypt, to his own people."

Abdul liked this idea. Reilly favored it as well. Jennifer had no choice but to agree. Besides she had been under tremendous emotional strain, and bringing SUM VII back to the hospital would take the responsibility of his care off her shoulders.

"These calculations," Reilly said, "this figuring that you found at the cabin. What do you make of it?"

I shrugged. "I saw the hieroglyphs. The rest of it could have been Greek. I don't know."

"And you say some of the sketches looked like orbits, perhaps even celestial maps?"

I nodded. "In some crazy way I think they were similar to some of the maps you might find at the observatory."

"Jennifer?"

She shrugged. "Twice I found him working on them in the cabin. I was never sure what they were all about."

Reilly thought for a long moment without speaking.

"The Egyptians had a tremendous fascination with astronomy," he said. "I wonder if SUM VII picked that cabin because he wanted to be close to the observatory. He may have discovered it by accident, but I think he chose to remain there for a specific reason. Perhaps he was trying to reorient himself, to locate the time period he is in. He has no other way to measure time. It would make sense that the observatory might be useful to him."

He looked at his watch. The sun had begun to set and evening was fast approaching. "The question now is how quickly we should act. I'm tempted to go to the cabin tonight, but it might be better to wait until dawn. Our best chance to get him back would be to slip in on him while he's asleep. We can post a couple of guards to watch the cabin throughout the night."

Reilly turned toward Jennifer.

"Do you think we could somehow coax him back to the hospital?"

"Perhaps I could try," she answered.

"No. Absolutely not!" I leaped from my seat. "It would be much too dangerous for you."

Reilly looked at her and smiled. "I'm afraid I agree." He nodded. "I want you as far away from him over the next twenty-four hours as possible. I meant the three of us, Bryan, myself, and Abdul."

She shrugged. "You might."

"Is that what you really think?"

She shook her head. "I think he'd rather die."

Reilly stood up slowly from his chair. "That is what I am afraid of," he said. "We'll contact the observatory first and then the police. If we're going to pull this off successfully we've still got much work to do."

26

WHEN WE reached the observatory, it was dark. Far below the city lights twinkled through a faint haze. The end of the day was gradually slipping away behind the western mountains.

A squad car with two police officers followed us into the parking lot, and the director of the observatory met us at the main gate. He was a thin man with hollow, sunken eyes.

In the lobby photographs of stellar objects hung along the walls. Some were of star clusters hundreds of thousands of light years away; some of whirling galaxies or tightly packed nebulas shining dimly from outer space. One photograph showed a comet blasting its way across the night; another the last remnants of a star, too distant to be seen by the naked eye.

The director led us into his office. His desk was cluttered with papers, but one page of calculations caught my eye. The mathematical symbols were different, but the writing, the computations, and the sketches were similar to the drawings at the cabin.

Reilly explained that we were searching for a man with an unusual interest in astronomy and asked if there had been any strange occurrences at the observatory.

"Funny you should ask," the director answered. "Last week we were doing some night photography, tracing one particularly faint galaxy. I had left the scope on an electronically controlled track that we'd computed the day before. When I came in the following morning, we found the telescope turned in a different direction. Our entire night's project was lost. There was no evidence of a break-in, and the gates were all locked in the morning just as they had been left the night before."

"Any problem since then?" Reilly asked.

"No. The gear has worked perfectly, although we haven't been able to accomplish much. Tonight is the first time since then that the weather prediction has been clear."

"And how easy would it be for someone to come in and change the direction of the scope?"

"Practically impossible," the director said. "First of all the person would have to get over the fence, which is twelve feet high and covered with barbed wire. Then we have two trained police dogs that are turned loose at night to patrol the grounds. They almost killed a couple of vandals a year ago. I doubt that anyone could get in. There are only two doors to the building, and both are closed and locked."

He led us out of the office and down along a corridor which opened into the huge observation room. Inside was the largest telescope I had even seen, held in place by a massive latticework of steel. The barrel was nearly twenty feet wide. It towered over us like a giant missile, pointing toward the domed ceiling a hundred feet above. Next to the telescope an electronic panel for tracking and locating stars filled one side of the room.

As the director spoke his words echoed off the walls.

"The position of the telescope is worked by a series of controls on these panels. Unless one has a thorough knowledge of computers, the telescope would be impossible to maneuver."

Reilly looked puzzled. "Perhaps an electronic malfunction?"

The director shook his head. "We reviewed the tapes in the morning. Somehow very precise tracking data had been programmed into the computer. The strange thing is that the tracking data was only half-finished. The telescope had been directed toward two completely opposite areas, one on grid ms-22sz, and a second on grid st-11bx. Two very distant galaxies, hundreds of light years apart. A third and fourth grid had been programmed but never used."

"How do you explain it?" Reilly asked.

"Our visibility index indicates that until two-fifteen in the morning there were scattered clouds. At two-thirty fog cover came over the mountains and obscured everything. From our calculations the telescopic tracking began at one-forty-five. Perhaps it was all coincidence," the director answered, "but I am not so sure."

By nine o'clock I was sitting in police headquarters waiting for Professor Reilly to come out. Abdul had remained at the observatory with the two officers to watch the cabin. We would join him later.

Some things about SUM VII were slowly beginning to fit into place. I could begin to see where the pieces should go, but I couldn't put them all together. Although Jennifer had supplied many of the answers concerning his disappearance, there were still many questions about the man. He seemed so tremendously different from the rest of us. The one thing that might help tie everything together could be the third language, the strange, musical, birdlike words SUM VII had spoken in his delirium. But what about the cellulose on the hemoglobin molecule and the radiocarbon dating of 27,000 years?

Each step of the way SUM VII had been a jump ahead of us. If he gave up and came to the hospital, everything would be fine, but I knew this would never happen. I just hoped no one would get hurt. At least Jennifer was safe. I had taken her home earlier in the evening and given her strict instructions to remain locked in her apartment for the night.

As we waited I watched one of the officers clean a long blue rifle. It looked like a gun which might be used to shoot big game. Only the bullets were different. Instead of having lead tips, each bullet was a dart with a hollow chamber inside that carried a potent sedative. It was the type of ammunition game collectors use to capture wild animals.

An aide waved for me to come inside. "Looks like they've got your man," he said.

I leaped to my feet just as Reilly and one of the policemen burst out of the office and ran for the door.

"Bring the anesthetic rifle," the police sergeant shouted. "We'll need two squad cars."

I spun around and raced after them. "What's happening?" I cried.

"I'm not sure," Reilly answered, a terrible frown on his face. "Abdul called to say he heard a shot. He had left the two officers at the cabin."

There was no time to be wasted. The squad cars pulled away from the sidewalk in a long accelerating screech, their sirens echoing wildly into the night.

I wondered if they had killed SUM VII.

27

ABDUL WAS waiting for us at the gate of the observatory. "Bad news, very bad news," he said.

We followed him quickly toward the cabin. The footing was difficult, the pathway obscured by shadows. Despite a slim quarter moon the mountains let little light into the valley.

A faint glow from the cabin came through the trees. Reilly and I moved in behind the police officer with the rifle. The rest of the men fanned out around the cabin. Through the window we could see the bed and part of the desk. At first I thought there was no one there.

Abdul pushed through the door. For a moment the room seemed empty, then I noticed two men dressed in officers' uniforms standing stiffly in the corner. They stared blankly across the cabin, scarcely breathing.

"Officer Blaire? Pilcher?" the policeman with the rifle cried.

He rushed up to them and passed a hand in front of their eyes. They did not blink. One still held a pistol, pointing it toward the floor.

They reminded me of the poor hospital guard. Now there were two more bodies for the psychiatrists to study. Their minds were completely blown.

We searched through the cabin. The pages of computations were gone. Low on one wall was a bullet which had dug into the wood.

A policeman reached down with a knife and dug the bullet out. There was no sign of blood and it appeared to have been a wild shot.

One of the other deputies had been attending the two men. "Look at his gun," he suddenly exclaimed.

He reached forward and pulled the revolver from the officer's hand. The striking thing was the disfigurement of the barrel. The metal had been melted and was twisted over upon itself.

When we brought the two officers back to the observatory, I could see the fear in the night guard's eyes as he tried to comprehend what had happened.

Abdul was grim and silent, the usual glint to his eye gone. "He must have caught them inside the cabin," he shook his head. "I should have never left them alone. I should have been there."

"Thank God you weren't," Reilly exclaimed. "It's my fault. I never should have let any of you come out here."

We waited at the observatory until the ambulance arrived and the attendants loaded the two officers into the van. They picked up the policemen as though they were statues and lay each upon a stretcher before the ambulance started up and disappeared into the valley. Its siren echoed hollowly off the mountains.

The saliva stuck to the back of my throat. For the first time we began to see SUM VII as alien and extremely dangerous. It had been naive to think he would react in friendly fashion. We had delivered him from his terminal sleep into a strange world where he had no allies, no friends. It was clear that he was determined not to come back to the hospital.

"I've got one more thought," Reilly finally said. "We'll have to hope he comes to the observatory tonight. It's a long shot, but it's the only chance we have left. The stacks of computations were missing from the cabin. If Jennifer is right, if he is indeed dying, I don't think he'll try to go too far."

28

THE NIGHT guard admitted us at the gate of the observatory. Inside the building Reilly stationed two men in each corridor. "Our plan will be to let him enter, then surround him and close in."

"Doubt anyone can get by the dogs," the guard grunted.

Reilly looked at Abdul. I knew what he was thinking. Somebody had got past them before.

As we took out final stations, Abdul drew Reilly aside. "I am thinking I would like to stand at the eastern doorway," he said. "The door which opens out into the woods."

"All right," Reilly answered, "I'll put two men with you."

Abdul held up his hand. "In all respect, sir. I am thinking I would best stand guard alone."

Reilly frowned. "You're not even armed," he said.

Abdul smiled and patted the side of his hip. The faint bulge of his long scimitarlike blade stuck out from his clothes. "I will be safe," he answered.

"All right," Reilly answered, "but I don't like it."

Abdul disappeared down the corridor with a funny look on his face, as though he had not heard the professor at all. I never felt safer than when Abdul was around, yet I wondered how even he might fare in a confrontation with SUM VII.

In the central corridor we checked the communications system through small hand-held radios. The professor and I walked to the main room of the observatory and sat down. The room was like a huge cave. The slightest sound echoed off the walls. The telescope towered massively above us, while across the room faint lights glowered upon the display panel. A constant low hum came from the electronic gear.

"I haven't felt like this since we were in the Hall of the Colossus," Reilly said. "Remind you of that?"

"Yes," I answered quietly.

"Think we've got a chance?"

"I'm not sure."

He coughed quietly in the darkness. I remained silent.

After a while he said, "It's going to be difficult to keep the police from shooting. If we miss him tonight, I think we've probably lost him for good. The paralyzed arm which Jennifer described bothers me a great deal. I'm sure he has started to hemorrhage inside his brain. I wonder if the episode in the museum might have triggered the bleeding."

"You mean when I chased him?"

"Yes," he answered. "The neurologists have said any rise in blood pressure would be dangerous. He's like a man walking around carrying a loaded bomb in his brain. Perhaps that is one of the reasons he does not want to come back. He may know that he is dying."

For the first time Reilly's confidence seemed to have ebbed away, leaving him upset and unsure. "These past several hours I've begun to regret everything we have done," he said.

I tried to be encouraging. "I'm not so sure," I answered. "We've learned a lot, and if we get him back safely, everything may turn out all right."

A check came over the two-way radio. The east and west corridors had seen nothing. The front entrance was intact and locked. There was no sign of unusual activity. In the distance a coyote howled, the sound drifting faintly through the observatory walls. Somewhere in the mountains the call was answered.

"Sometimes I think science moves too slowly," Reilly said. "But when something like this happens, I know that slow, deliberate progress is necessary. It takes nature hundreds and thousands of years to work some things out. We try things prematurely and we make mistakes."

There was a faint click on the two-way radio. A

voice came over in a whisper. "Got some movement outside. West wall."

We waited in silence. The huge vault of the observatory loomed above us. The tracking gear glowed steadily. A coyote howled again.

Five minutes passed before there was another click on the radio. "Footsteps . . ." the voice said. "West wall. Coming close . . ."

Reilly stood up and directed me to take off my shoes. "Try not to make a noise." He moved quickly across the room and along the wall toward the western corridor. At the end of the hallway a faint light shone through a window high on the wall. We crept silently toward it. One of the policemen made a low warning noise with his teeth as we came up behind him.

The footsteps on the other side of the wall were irregular. A few steps, a pause, then more steps, all the time coming closer. After a scuffling noise the footsteps became fainter.

One of the officers let out a long sigh. He had been holding his breath. I started to say something when the policeman in front of me held up his hand. The footsteps were returning, coming slowly toward the door. Then they stopped. Somebody was right outside!

The officer behind me raised the rifle while a second officer glided toward the door.

"Get ready," he whispered.

We waited for an eternity in the darkness.

"Now!" he cried. Suddenly the door was flung open. Teeth flashed, and there was a horrible throaty roar. For a second the nightmare in the museum descended upon me again, the mask with the terrible eyes, the shiny, jagged teeth lunging toward me. Then the door slammed and we were left in darkness. A ferocious barking erupted outside.

Reilly cursed quietly. It was a dog, one of the German shepherds that patrolled the grounds. We had forgotten all about them.

In a few moments the night guard could be heard running along the pavement. He arrived at the door, breathing heavily.

"Hold off, Jynx," he yelled. "Everything all right in there?"

One of the officers opened the door. "Mistook your dog for our man," he said. "Everything is okay. Sorry we blew it."

He turned on the lights and inspected the area. I looked at Professor Reilly. For the first time in a week he was grinning.

"Well, Christ, if we ever scared him off, we sure did then," he sighed. "Let's turn out the lights and return to our posts."

I followed him back to the main observatory. The experience had shattered my nerves, leaving my legs unsteady.

Reilly checked over the radio with Abdul. Everything was quiet along the eastern corridor. It was almost midnight.

"Why don't we try to get some sleep," Reilly said. "We can cover in shifts. I'll wake you at three."

I nodded halfheartedly, not sure whether I could fall asleep. Finally I curled up in the corner and tried to make a small pillow out of my jacket. The stone floor was hard and cold. Yet I must have been more tired than I thought, for in a few minutes I drifted into a fitful, restless sleep.

I awoke several times with cramps in my back, thinking how uncomfortable the floor was. No position was better than any other. At two-thirty I checked my watch before falling back to sleep.

A viselike grip on my right arm woke me. I started to move but the vise tightened. The professor was crouched next to me. He had grabbed my arm and was trying to hold me still. Slowly I raised to a sitting position. He bent over, his mouth close to my ear.

"Someone is here," he whispered.

As he spoke a shadow passed in front of the lights on the display panel. I stared into the darkness.

Where were the officers? Where was Abdul? How could anyone have gotten into the room past the dogs?

With a grinding noise a huge door began to slide across the dome of the observatory. The night sky flooded into the room and the light from a thousand stars blinked out of the darkness. The noise changed, a gear shifted. The entire dome rotated above us, revolving fifteen degrees in a counterclockwise direction before stopping.

In the faint starlight a figure glided toward the base of the telescope. Footsteps rang on metal stairs. The figure had begun to climb a small ladder which led up to an observation station halfway up the telescope.

"It's got to be him," Reilly whispered.

We waited in silence. The figure reached the top of the ladder and hunched down next to a sighting piece on the main scope. A tiny light flashed on, and the machinery started up again. The dome rotated another ten degrees, as the angle of the telescope changed.

Then, without warning, we heard a moan which gradually increased to a wail of lamentation. This was followed by a lesser cry, clearly one of pain. With a crash the figure, half-sliding, half-falling, slipped down the ladder and plunged to the floor.

At the same moment lights flooded the observatory. One of the officers stood by the light switch, his gun drawn. A second officer was holding a rifle while two others slowly advanced from the doorway.

I turned toward the man who had fallen down the ladder. It was SUM VII a look of terrible anguish on his face. He was cradling the side of his head in his left hand. His right arm was trailing uselessly by his side.

"It's the aneurysm," Reilly yelled, moving directly in front of the officers. "Don't shoot," he cried. "Hold your fire."

As SUM VII half-crouched to face us, I was not sure he recognized who we were. When his eyes finally focused, he dropped his hand and stood erect. For a second his eyes seemed to glow a dull red, then a sudden burning in my head made me cry out. Everything became white. My brain was exploding. I don't know how long the pain lasted, but it must have been only a second, for when I regained my senses SUM VII had slumped to the floor. His eyes, half-open, were staring in the direction of the electronic panel.

A sharp explosion erupted from the console, followed by a second and then a third. Flames shot up from the panel. The discharges showered off the console, starting up secondary blazes on the computer board. It was as if SUM VII could no longer control his thoughts, and bolts of energy were spontaneously escaping from his mind.

I rushed forward. Clearly he was dying. For a moment he was overcome by a small convulsion, then he tried to raise his head. Words poured from his mouth in the strange musical language which none of us could understand. I wanted to assist him but was helpless.

Reilly yelled for someone to get a fire extinguisher. From various parts of the building came scattered shouts and the sound of running feet. Separate blazes still sprang up on the console, igniting further explosions as the circuits became overheated and fired.

A faint frown crossed SUM VII's face. For one moment I thought that he recognized me. Then a long gasping sigh escaped his lips. His eyes closed, his muscles eased. A firm hand reached across my shoulder and pulled me gently away.

"Let him go," Reilly said softly. "He's been through enough. Let him go in peace."

A cry of terrible anguish rose in my throat, a cry of loss, of frustration, of failure. In the weird illumination of the electronic fires the Egyptian's face looked the way it had when we first unwrapped him. His shirt was open at the top, the delicate blue necklace still around his neck. He took one more breath and tried to mumble something; then his head fell back and he was gone.

Reilly bent forward and felt for his pulse. It had stopped. When he reached forward and pried open the Egyptian's eyes, the left pupil was widely dilated, the right small. The aneurysm had finally broken loose. He had hemorrhaged inside the brain.

I looked around the room. Policemen were scurrying back and forth spraying foam upon the fire. But something was wrong. Something was missing.

"Abdul?" I gasped. "Where is Abdul?"

"My God," Reilly cried. "Eastern corridor."

We raced toward it. The door at the end of the

hallway was open, and a faint orange glow from outside indicated dawn was approaching.

"Oh, Christ, oh, no," I thought. Abdul must have
tried to stop SUM VII. Beyond the doorway I saw
something that made my heart stand still. Standing on
the edge of a steep ravine the immobile silhouette of a
man was caught in the growing light.

"Abdul!" I shouted. But there was no answer.

I sprinted frantically to his side. The figure, a massive block of granite, was staring off across the valley.

Suddenly Abdul's eyes blinked, and his lips spread
in the thinnest smile. "Is everything all right?" he said
in a quiet voice.

I nodded and gave a tremendous sigh of relief. "But
then . . . then you must have seen him," I exclaimed.
"You must have let him through."

"He has made an incredible journey, Mr. St. John,"
Abdul answered slowly. "I am thinking it is time we
take him home."

29

THE LAST three months have rocketed by in such a blur that it's hard to put everything in perspective. It is seven in the morning. Already sweat is pouring down my face. I cannot escape the Egyptian sun. Even Jennifer, with her beautiful figure and flowing blond hair, seems limp and exhausted.

Last night, sleeping underneath the stars in the Valley of the Sphinx, we lay awake for a long time staring at the universe. Millions of stars sparkled in the Egyptian night, and beyond them were entire galaxies so distant that they burned as one collective pinpoint of light. And beyond that . . . the infinities.

Then SUM VII flashed across my mind like some brilliant meteor, surpassing the illumination of all the heavenly lights. We have laid him to rest this very morning in the Valley of the Sphinx. We have come fifteen thousand miles, at a cost of fifty-one thousand dollars, to return the body of the Egyptian to his tomb in the rock and the sands.

Just before dawn the coffin was pulled down the passageway and gently lowered into the hidden crypt beneath the Hall of the Colossus. Like superstitious priests Abdul and the professor carefully mortared the stone floor so that it could not be lifted. Then we dynamited the entrance to the tomb amid great clouds of smoke and dust. Its location has been carefully recorded, but all of its treasures have been removed. No grave robber will ever again gain entrance to the passageway.

As the last dust settled, Abdul climbed along the face of the cliff to seal the opening used by the bats. When he returned we loaded our equipment onto the camels that had been waiting restlessly. Everyone was eager to get back to Luxor. Even now we have much ground to cover before the sun becomes so hot that travel is impossible.

Yet these are peculiar actions for scientific men. They are peculiar for a professor of anatomy with over one hundred papers and three textbooks to his credit. They are peculiar for a world-renowned cardiac surgeon whose funds paid for the present expedition. And they are peculiar even for me, a medical student, and my bride of fifteen days. It is a strange honeymoon we have taken, but Jennifer insisted on it. Having seen the end of SUM VII, she wanted to see where it all began.

Abdul rides at the front of the caravan scanning the horizon. He does not talk. He has long ago learned that some things are beyond the comprehension of man. Mystified are the dozen fellahin who have come with us to assist in the unloading and the sealing of the tomb. They are from peasant villages and do not understand the unorthodox ways of American scientists. They shake their heads and mutter at one another in disbelief.

For what value is a useless piece of flesh that has been buried for five thousand years? What use can there possibly be in reburying the very thing that we spent so much time and effort in digging up?

At first it would seem that sentimentality had overtaken us, that our own guilt was so great that we could no longer live with a desecrated grave. Yet it is the scientific explanation of SUM VII that brought us back to Egypt.

As we passed the entrance to the valley, I glanced back at the sphinxlike outcropping for the last time. I have seen and felt things associated with this place that I will never forget. Hopefully SUM VII will be safe here. We talked for many hours about placing the body in a museum or some type of storage vault. Yet in the total scheme of history these places seemed fragile and transitory. Who could guarantee that a museum would stand for another five thousand years? Governments, politics, and people change. The Egyptian sands do not. Only here SUM VII's grave seems secure for it is unlikely that anyone will ever come here again.

The computer translations were our first key. It took the linguistics laboratory forty-five days to work out the meaning of the five, possibly six, paragraphs of unknown language that escaped SUM VII's lips during his delirium.

We could only conclude that this was his native speech. We had looked for something in the past, some clue that might connect the words with early Egyptian or even another language of the time. But whenever we tried to solve the problem, the computer responded with the same answer.

LANGUAGE UNKNOWN. NO REFERENCE TO LAN-
GUAGE SYSTEMS KNOWN TO EXIST TIME PERIOD
1000 TO 10,000 B.C.

We searched further. The radiocarbon dating indicated that the body of SUM VII was 27,000 years old. Twenty to thirty thousand years ago was the time when Cro-Magnon man inhabited caves during the last great advance of ice. It was the time when the great hairy mastodon roamed through North America, when man first began to make his charcoal drawings on the caves in France. For forty-five days we got nowhere until Spanzerelli, in exasperation, fed the third language of SUM VII into the computer and asked for a comparison to any language. The print-out returned in fifteen seconds.

LANGUAGE ROOTS NOT COMPARABLE TO ANY
KNOWN WORLD LANGUAGE INCLUDING MAJOR
GROUPINGS: RUSSIAN, ENGLISH, JAPANESE, ARA-
BIC, FRENCH. PHONETIC SYLLABLES ENGLISH,
EGYPTIAN. LANGUAGE III SHOWS NUMERICAL
TREND.

"What the hell?" Spanzerelli frowned. He went back and listened to the tapes again, this time writing down the phonetic passages and laboriously counting each of the sounds.

Suddenly he saw it. "My God!" he cried. "What a fool I have been. It is exactly how Champollion translated the Rosetta Stone. The phonetic groupings of certain passages are the same. He has taken the English, translated it into early Egyptian, and then to Language III. His mind works exactly like a computer. For three of the passages the words are different, but the meaning is exactly the same."

By now Professor Reilly and Dr. Beeson had arrived and we all gathered around the computer trying to piece together what Spanzerelli had found.

He was so excited that his hands trembled at the keyboard. He added the instructions:

COMPARE PASSAGES WITH EQUAL NUMBER OF WORDS. USE ENGLISH PASSAGES TO KEY CONNOTATIONS.

Lights flashed upon the computer. Tapes spun wildly. The computer responded in two and a half minutes.

PASSAGES COMPARED. LOCKING COMPLETED.

Spanzerelli leaped to his feet. "I think we got it!" he yelled. My pulse quickened, Reilly stood up, Beeson's jaw dropped slightly, and Spanzerelli's hands flashed across the keyboard. In a frenzy he pounded in the instructions.

BABEL PROGRAM. TRANSLATE: PASSAGE SUM VII LANGUAGE TYPE III ACCORDING TO WORD COMPARISONS ENGLISH/EGYPTIAN. ENGLISH, WRITTEN MODE.

We turned on the audio portion of the tape. We could hear SUM VII's voice in his delirium, crying out in the strange musical language. Gasping he muttered one phrase after the next. As he spoke the computer began rattling out a printout faster than the eye could read.

PASSAGE I. BABEL PROGRAM. SUM VII LANGUAGE
TYPE III/ENGLISH TRANSLATION. PRINT MODE.
PRINT ENGLISH.

ORBITING PATHWAY ALTERED. LOSING SPEED. TRA-
JECTORY SINKING. ASSISTANCE . . . ASSISTANCE
. . . ASSISTANCE . . .

COMPUTER CORRECTION. "ASSISTANCE" POSSIBLE
ERROR. OTHER SYNONYMS: HELP, AID, SUPPORT.

CONNOTATION CHECK: KEY WORDS. ORBIT, SPEED,
TRAJECTORY ALTERNATIVE: DISTRESS SIGNAL,
"MAYDAY," INSERT MAYDAY. DELETE ASSISTANCE.

PASSAGE II. BABEL PROGRAM. SUM VII LANGUAGE
TYPE III/ENGLISH TRANSLATION. PRINT MODE.
PRINT ENGLISH.

ORBITING PATHWAY ALTERED. LOSING SPEED. TRA-
JECTORY SINKING . . . MAYDAY . . . MAYDAY . . .
MAYDAY . . .

We watched the printout, scarcely breathing. Each
message repeated the same words, the same call for
help.

And now it became incredibly clear. SUM VII was
not from Egypt. Somehow he had been caught in some
terrible accident and had crashed in the sands. He had
split his crew and they had been lost upon the desert.
By a stroke of luck he had been found by the Egyptians, who recognized him as a man of miraculous
powers. He could not have been considered otherwise.
It was only natural that he would have been made a
high priest.

I wondered if somehow SUM VII might have in-
fluenced the Egyptian custom of mummification and
burial of the dead. Buried in a stone crypt hidden
away from the rest of the world, he might remotely
hope for rescue by his own people. His cells were so
structured that once circulation stopped they would
become dormant. It was an ideal state for the passage

of great time required for space travel. Now the peculiar characteristic of the hemoglobin molecule and the preservation of the cells made sense. But what time must have passed! If the computer and our radiocarbon dating were correct, he and his crew must have been traveling for more than twenty thousand years. That assumed he had come from an atmosphere similar to ours. If not the radiocarbon dating was meaningless. It could have been twenty thousand or two hundred thousand years.

A rush of questions flashed through my mind. The hieroglyphic writing, the strange stone monuments, the great pyramids, the pantheon of weird animal-headed gods. Did Egypt really spring out of a primitive society of mud huts, or had there been assistance from a race far older and wiser than ourselves?

How stupid and naive we had been to boast of our incredible resuscitation! No wonder he had wanted to escape our hospital. Medical science in the twentieth century must have been as primitive to him as medicine from the Dark Ages seems to us. Our treatment of him would have been no different from being in the clutches of medieval barbers, who trephined away your skull or siphoned off your blood. In all of our scientific exuberance we had merely delayed his rest, derailed his plans.

Yet one more thing still bothered me. SUM VII had climbed the stairwell at the observatory and made numerous adjustments on the telescope presumably looking for some remote star in the heavens of the night. Something he had seen up there on the top of the platform had caused him to utter his anguished cry, his great lamentation of despair.

The following night the director of the observatory went back and traced the computer tracking, following the exact course which SUM VII had scanned as he searched through the telescope. At 4:36 precisely, the time he had been upon the platform, Reilly, Abdul, and I, each in turn, looked through the eyepiece into the blackness of space. At the very farthest reach of our vision was a tiny galaxy no bigger than a minute pinwheel. I saw it for but a second before it was obscured by a hundred thousand brighter lights.

I knew then what SUM VII must have felt as he searched the night, and what one of our own astronauts might someday experience as he looks longingly for our sun from the shores of a planet thousands of light years away. He was a wayward voyager seeking some sign of rescue in the night. For SUM VII, five thousand years had passed and there was only the deafening silence of the stars to mark them. What futility! What despair!

I do not think I will ever want to go back to Egypt again. There are things about life and death there that I am no longer curious to ask. For me death will be a journey into the unknown. For SUM VII it is something else. If he is lucky, if the geography of Egypt does not change, if his tomb remains safe, then one day a strange ship might come nosing through our galaxy looking for certain telltale signs of life.

And so we buried him, there where we found him, where the hieroglyphic paintings said he was a man out of the Nubian wastes, a man who could "calm wild beasts" and "turn a man to stone." Inside his coffin the Egyptians had painted the figure of Nut, the goddess of the night. Her head lay upon his head, her arms covered his arms, her legs atop his legs. Over his shoulder the small fluttering owl which carried off the soul was carved into the stone. Someday, the legends said, his soul would return again to his body for its final rest.

"It's a strange paradox, Mr. St. John," Abdul once told me across the campfire in the Valley of the Sphinx. "Sometimes to see the future, we must go back to the most remote and distant past."

KEEP YOURSELF IN SUSPENSE...

from
BALLANTINE BOOKS

Bestsellers from BALLANTINE